A HUSBAND TO BELONG TO

Susan Fox

D0039232

TORONTO • NEW YORK • LONDON
AMSTERDAM • PARIS • SYDNEY • HAMBURG
STOCKHOLM • ATHENS • TOKYO • MILAN • MADRID
PRAGUE • WARSAW • BUDAPEST • AUCKLAND

ISBN 0-373-03881-X

A HUSBAND TO BELONG TO

First North American Publication 2006.

Copyright © 2005 by Susan Fox.

This edition published by arrangement with Harlequin Books S.A.

® and TM are trademarks of the publisher. Trademarks indicated with ® are registered in the United States Patent and Trademark Office, the Canadian Trade Marks Office and in other countries.

www.eHarlequin.com

Printed in U.S.A.

The tender kiss was persuasive. Whatever Marla had thought Jess's lips might feel like, it was nothing compared to this—warm, firm, caressing.

He released her hands and his arms came around her, but his lips stayed gentle, coaxing. She belatedly thought about pulling away—there was still time to keep this brief!—but it was at that moment that his lips surged hotly against hers, and he pulled her against him so tightly she could feel both their heartbeats.

For the first time in her life, Marla felt powerful. A feminine confidence she'd never had before rose up. Jess had kissed her, and now he was out of breath. Jess Craddock, macho tough guy, was now trembling in her arms! It didn't matter that she was just as out of breath and as shaken as he was.

Susan Fox figures she's lived enough of her life in the city to consider moving back to the country. Her country dream home would include a few pygmy goats to take care of the lawn, a couple of ponies for granddaughters Arissa and Emma, a horse or two for herself and whatever stray cats or dogs might happen by looking for a home. Until then, she fears she'll have to make do with a lawn mower, three always-up-to-something cats and two very naughty but adorable stray kittens.

Susan loves to hear from her fans. You can contact her via her Web site www.susanfox.org

CHAPTER ONE

THE two young women didn't look like sisters, much less like fraternal twins, though DNA testing had confirmed their genetic bond. In almost every other way they were opposites, in looks as well as personality and upbringing.

Jaicey Craddock, older by two minutes, had blue eyes and wavy blond hair that had been streaked brighter by the Texas sun. Her tan set off her coloring, and her sanguine personality had been influenced as much by her adoptive family as it had been by the optimism she seemed to have been born with.

Her sister, Marla Norris, was a full inch shorter than she was, and her manner was as reserved as Jaicey's was outgoing. Marla's mink-brown hair was thick and straight, and had been cut to fall sleekly to her shoulders. Her wispy bangs drew more attention to her soft hazel eyes than she was aware of, and the years of keeping her feelings hidden showed in her aloof gaze, lending her a mystery that made her seem older and wiser than her sister.

Marla had been just as shaped by the hard times that had dominated her growing up years as Jaicey had been by the happy ones so prevalent in hers. Unlike Jaicey, Marla had lost her adoptive parents by the time she'd turned eight. She'd also lost what was left of her childhood, changed by shock and grief into a wary girl who'd endured a small series of foster placements and learned to survive the loneliness of not belonging and never truly feeling secure.

She'd had to create those things for herself, and she'd worked hard at it. After graduating high school, Marla had become ruthlessly self-sufficient, leery of depending on anyone but herself. She'd shunned the "mirages" of rescue that lost children dreamed of and some grown women looked to a man to provide.

It was safer that way. You couldn't be disappointed or used if you didn't put much hope or faith in other people. And if you didn't allow yourself to get too close to anyone, you couldn't be traumatized by abandonment when it came, or emotional drama. The only real price she'd paid to be free of troubles like those was that she sometimes felt lonely and unfulfilled.

Until the sister she'd never dreamed existed had breezed into her life and changed it forever.

"Are you sorry I talked you into moving to Texas?"

Jaicey's question broke the companionable silence they'd fallen into as they finished with the photo albums they'd been putting together at the kitchen table in

Marla's apartment. They'd spent every evening that week working on them, trading extra copies of school photos and ones they'd taken themselves over the years.

What had got them started on this project was the craving to fill in some of the first twenty-four years of life together that they'd missed out on. Plus, they'd bought the lion's share of the professional photographs Jaicey had insisted they have taken a month ago, and they'd needed a place to display the smaller ones they'd picked.

The question made Marla look over at Jaicey to see traces of uncharacteristic worry in her eyes.

"Never," Marla said, and meant it. It still amazed her that she'd packed up everything she owned three months ago and moved from Illinois to live in Coulter City, Texas, but she couldn't imagine ever regretting it.

Jaicey still looked troubled. "Not even knowing we have to keep the biggest secret of our lives for a while longer?"

"If I had misgivings, I wouldn't have moved all this way."

Now the shadows in Jaicey's beautiful eyes faded. "So if I asked you to come to the ranch this weekend, you'd say yes?"

"I'm a little less sure of that."

Jaicey grinned. "Still nervous around my big brother, huh?" she guessed. "That's called sexual attraction, little sister."

Marla felt her face warm. No one but Jaicey had ever detected her feelings so easily, and it still caught her a little off guard.

"Maybe," she allowed, "but the more time I spend around your family, the more opportunities we have to slip up."

"And you're not comfortable dodging questions." Now the worry was back in Jaicey's eyes. "I don't like keeping things from them, either."

"That, too," Marla agreed.

Not to mention that Jaicey's older brother, Jake Craddock, was usually the one asking questions. No matter how she answered him, she somehow managed to make him more suspicious of her than ever.

And yet his suspicion had been clear to Marla the moment Jaicey had introduced her to the Craddocks. Judd had been happy to meet her, welcoming her without reservation, but Jake had given her such a hard, searching look before he'd eventually smiled and said all the polite words, that she hadn't been able to keep herself from getting away from him as soon as she reasonably could.

Since then he'd managed to find things to ask her about, no matter how hard she tried to keep from attracting his attention. Though she'd always been good at keeping a low profile, Jake was frustratingly hard to avoid. If Jaicey hadn't been around to distract him from playing Twenty Questions or to chide him for it, Marla wasn't certain she would have been fast enough to come up with reasonable answers that weren't spur-of-the-moment lies.

She hated lies, but Jake was so good at probing into areas she didn't want to account for that it was a challenge to answer and tell the truth, or at least as much of the truth as she could. After their first encounter, she'd gone home and brainstormed possible future questions, trying to formulate true but uninformative answers, along with a few little evasions, just in case.

Now anytime Marla went for a visit to Craddock Ranch, she was taking the risk that she might unintentionally give Jake a clue to figure things out before Jaicey could advance her careful campaign to confess. Even worse, he might somehow get her to blab their secret. He seemed to have a knack for scrambling her emotions as well as her brain, which made her even more reluctant to be around him. Marla didn't want to be the one who gave the secret away.

Jaicey was afraid to just baldly confess to Jake and his father that she'd gone looking for her birth mother and come home with a sister. Judd and Jake were sticklers for loyalty, so they might think that what Jaicey had done was disloyal.

Or ungrateful. Judd and his late wife, Nona, had given Jaicey everything a little girl could want, especially love, and Jaicey didn't want him to think that what they'd done for her hadn't been good enough. A lot of adoptive parents were hurt by what might look like disloyalty or ingratitude, and Marla couldn't blame them for feeling insecure, at least for a while. On top of that, Judd Craddock's health hadn't been too good the past couple of years, so Jaicey didn't want to shock him.

Her plan was to gradually lead up to it. Jaicey was sure there'd be a right time and place, but she was determined in the meantime for her family to get to know Marla. Jaicey was convinced they'd greet her confession better if they already liked her new "best friend." Marla wasn't at all confident of that.

She wouldn't have done things this way if she'd been in Jaicey's place, and she felt guilty for not thinking more clearly about the consequences of her sister's plan. It would have been better if she'd stayed in Chicago until things had been worked out with the Craddocks, but after Jaicey had repeatedly urged her to move to Texas, Marla couldn't have refused if her life had depended on it. Now that she'd lived here for a few weeks and loved it, the only thing she regretted was that she felt compelled to keep a secret of this magnitude.

She should have known better than to let Jaicey talk her into going to the ranch that first time, but she'd been as carried away by curiosity about the Craddocks and the need to know everything about her sister as Jaicey had been eager to bring her whole family together.

They should have told the Craddocks weeks ago. After

all this time they were sure to be angry once they knew, whether they ever showed that anger to Jaicey or not.

Jaicey was the one they loved, and Marla had no doubt that any upset they felt about the revelation would be directed far more toward her than Jaicey. Their first thought would likely be that Marla had been the one who'd wanted to keep things secret for a while.

They might even believe that she'd influenced Jaicey to be disloyal by keeping a secret from them so long. To the Craddocks, family members never "took sides" against each other. It was also possible they'd think she'd been the one to approach Jaicey instead of the other way around, no matter what Jaicey told them now.

That was the problem with keeping a secret this big. The worst part was that once it was revealed, the Craddock's trust in Jaicey might be affected long into the future, and Marla worried about that.

Craddock was a big name in Texas, with the holdings and the fortune that went with it. Marla already knew from her sister that more than one opportunist had targeted each of the Craddocks in the past. Though Marla's pride was outraged at the idea that anyone would consider her an opportunist, it wouldn't be unheard of from people who'd learned to be skeptical of strangers.

Perhaps that was why Jake was so suspicious of her friendship with his sister. Jaicey was an heiress, and Marla was a nobody with only a few thousand dollars in savings. Maybe once he found out the truth, Jake would think Marla had been motivated more by Craddock money than a true wish to be reunited with her sister.

If he did, he'd find out soon enough that he was wrong. She'd had plenty of time these past months to exploit Jaicey's natural generosity. Marla had been on guard against it from the beginning, particularly after she'd had car trouble and her sister had tried to buy her a new car. She'd adamantly refused, then found herself refusing other gifts, even going so far as to make Jaicey return some jewelry and clothes she'd bought.

Jaicey hadn't been happy about any of that, but she'd finally understood Marla meant what she said about paying her own way. Marla had even set a spending limit on birthday and Christmas gifts, which Jaicey still complained about.

The only thing she'd allowed Jaicey to do for her was to give her a personal reference for the job she'd taken as a secretary with a Coulter City law firm. Surely the Craddocks wouldn't find fault with that.

Jaicey stood then and started to reach for the briefcase she'd set on a kitchen chair.

"I mean it, Marlie," she was saying. "I want you to come to the ranch this weekend. I have a feeling this visit might make a big difference between you and Jake."

Marla wasn't exactly relieved by that idea. She'd just as soon keep her distance from Jake for the time being, but she didn't comment.

Jaicey picked up her photo album and put it in the

case while Marla slid the scraps and snippets they'd trimmed from the photos into a single pile to throw away later.

"By the way, he won't be asking nosy questions anymore."

Marla glanced over, alert to the hint in what her sister had said. Jaicey was grinning as if she was pleased with herself, and Marla searched her expression warily.

"What did you do?"

"I told Jake to stop nagging you. He's always had a thing for mysterious women who don't come onto him, so I reminded him of that, too."

Marla was horrified. "You didn't!" Jaicey waved away her reaction.

"So when he stops over to apologize, I hope you'll let him in. He's also going to invite you to the ranch for the weekend. We're all going camping, which is something else you haven't done, right?"

Marla's horror rose another notch. She already knew the Craddocks were outdoorsy people who not only worked outside, but also hunted and fished. She'd never in her life gone camping, which sounded like fun, but she'd rather not take that on with Jake around. She'd been self-conscious enough learning how to ride a horse on the weekends she'd gone to the ranch, and common sense warned there might be a lot less room to retreat from Jake if the four of them were pitching tents in the middle of nowhere.

"Ah, come on, Marlie," Jaicey coaxed, "you'll love it. Jake was the one who suggested you might like to go hunting for arrowheads. There must be dozens scattered around that no one's taken time to pick up. Maybe some pottery shards if we're lucky. And he thinks we've got another cougar, so we might do some tracking."

Despite her resistance to the idea of going to the ranch, Marla felt a spark of temptation. She had an interest in archeology, but no experience with it beyond reading magazines and watching TV programs. Though picking up a few arrowheads and pottery shards wasn't anything serious, it always excited her to think about finding something that remained of people who'd lived long ago. And the idea of tracking a cougar was tantalizing. Was there a chance of getting close enough to see it?

"I'll…think about it," Marla said. "But I don't have any camping gear." Jaicey waved that away, too.

"We've got equipment and bedrolls. All you'll need are riding clothes, boots and your Stetson. Sunblock if you want it, and hair ties. I'll loan you some gloves. Don't bother with makeup or more than basic toiletries, and *don't* bring a hair drier. You'd never live it down."

Marla smiled wryly. "I'm not such a city girl that I thought there'd be electricity on the range."

"Just makin' sure." Jaicey thumbed closed the latches on the briefcase and pulled it off the table. "And if I've timed this right, I can open the door for Jake on my way out the lobby."

Marla had been about to turn to go ahead of her sister into the living room, but she did a double-take when Jaicey's words dawned on her.

"Tonight?"

Jaicey ignored her dismay. "It has to be tonight. Tomorrow's Friday." She nodded toward the table. "You might want to put that photo album out of sight while you're at it."

A heartbeat later, her smile faded. Suddenly she set down her briefcase and impulsively grabbed Marla for a hard hug.

Marla automatically hugged back—something she'd rarely done before Jaicey had made it an almost daily part of her life. Jaicey's whisper sent a chill through her.

"I feel like there's no time for anything, Marlie, like I should have found you years ago. I know I'm pushing everything too fast, but I can't seem to help it."

There it was again, Jaicey's touching rush to make up for all the years they'd lost. She often seemed preoccupied with the notion of time, and it always gave Marla a shiver of unease because she felt the same way herself.

The hug tightened mutually before Jaicey relaxed her arms and drew back a little, blinking to clear her eyes of tears. Marla tried to do the same, but couldn't switch emotional gears that fast. Family love and affection were still too new, and since she didn't have many memories of those from childhood, she tended to cling to them longer than others might. Sisterly tears were even harder to keep in perspective. She still marveled that Jaicey loved her. There was no question she loved Jaicey.

"Besides," Jaicey went on, "it wouldn't break my heart if you and Jake fell for each other. A wedding would put us all together perfectly."

Marla felt the shock of that to her toes, and shook her head a little. "I feel like I've just been run over by a bus."

Jaicey giggled.

"I've got a knack for matchmaking, didn't I tell you? If I can get Daddy married off to the Widow Lane, then I'll be able to devote myself full-time to finding someone for Jake. If I happen to match you up with Jake while I'm workin' on Daddy, I'd take care of all three of you at once. Then I can finally let Bobby Kelsey lasso me for my own walk down the aisle."

Marla shook her head again, a little in wonder. Jaicey was like a glittering whirlwind that spun and skipped through the day, stirring things up with her energy, her good intentions and her zest for life. Of all the sisters she might have had, Marla considered Jaicey the ideal. Not only was she Marla's opposite, but she was also one of the most genuinely caring and fun people she'd ever known. When had she ever felt so lucky, so blessed?

The question made a smile of happiness burst up through the cheerful chaos her sister had made of her life.

"No one will ever accuse you of not having goals," Marla commented with a playfulness that was also new for her, "but please don't try to match me with your brother. We'd be terrible together," she added, hoping to put a gentle end to that idea. She couldn't imagine Jake Craddock marrying someone like her—she couldn't imagine marrying someone like him!

"Ha. My brother's also got a thing for brunettes, so be sure to brush that gorgeous hair, and tweak a little color into your cheeks so you don't look like you're about to faint. Jake isn't half as obnoxious as he pretends to be."

And then the blond whirlwind released her to snatch up the briefcase and glide into the living room to let herself out of the apartment. Before Jaicey closed the door all the way, she turned to push it open again and wink. "Love ya, Marlie."

Marla called out a bemused, "Love you, too," as Jaicey pulled the door closed. Marla stood staring at it a few seconds, then took a fortifying breath. Jake Craddock could be here any moment now, so she turned back to the photo album on the table.

Almost instantly, she felt a clench of anxiety. At first Marla thought it was because she would soon be alone with Jake. In those next seconds, she somehow knew he had nothing to do with this level of foreboding.

Marla shakily opened the album and felt her anxiety mount as she flipped through the series of photos until she came to the ones she liked best: the professional ones of her and Jaicey together, the first actual family portraits she remembered ever being part of.

She'd matted and framed the fourteen-by-seventeen of her favorite one herself, but it was sitting in her bedroom. Until the Craddocks knew everything, she was leery of hanging it in her living room where anyone could see it. Since Jake was supposed to stop by tonight, she was glad she'd been cautious.

The comfort she'd hoped for when she'd opened the album didn't come so she took it to the bedroom while she tried to distract herself from the sharpening sense of dread. At least she was dressed fairly well in the white blouse she'd worn to work that day and the pair of new jeans she'd changed into when she'd got home. Should she put on a pair of shoes, or were the trouser socks she had on okay?

She set the album on the dresser, checked her light makeup and brushed her hair, then glanced into the full-length mirror on the closet door to inspect her overall appearance. Her clothes were neat and were casual enough to make her look relaxed—though she was anything but relaxed—so she hurried to the living room to wait, determined to project a serene facade.

Surely Jake would only stay a few minutes. This was just a duty call that Jaicey had engineered, and he'd probably only agreed to come because she'd pestered him to. Marla didn't think for a moment that Jake Craddock would actually apologize, and she was certain his invitation—if he followed through with it—would be tersely spoken and uncomfortable, especially for her. This shouldn't take longer than ten minutes tops, and she could stand anything for ten minutes.

As she walked around the living room, adjusting a throw pillow and switching on a couple of lamps, she tried to force away her ongoing feeling of anxiety by thinking about something else. And of course, the first thing that came to mind was to wonder how Jake was taking the pressure their sister was putting on him to accept her.

Their sister. Never in her life had she suspected she'd had a sister before Jaicey had contacted her, especially not a fraternal twin. Then to find out she shared that sister with anyone else—much less Jake Craddock—and would for the rest of their lives, took even more getting used to.

Jaicey seemed to think the sun rose and set on her big brother. Marla might have agreed had she not been the person he'd taken an instant dislike to. And yet, she'd never known many men who were as protective as Jake was, and something inside her craved having all that protection on her side.

For more than half her life Marla had suppressed the longing for security that was focused on anyone but herself, but everything about Jake seemed to shout security, from his tough-guy looks to the closeness of his family.

Opening up to Jaicey had been the start of all this. The emotional reserve and prudent distance she'd learned to so rigidly maintain had been severely undermined, maybe permanently, and now she had to do her best to shore them up.

It was hard enough to do with Jaicey so involved in her life, and it was remarkably hard to do where Jake was concerned. Despite his mistrust of her and the way harsh men like him intimidated her, Marla also found he was nothing like the few city men she'd been around or dated, which might be part of the reason she couldn't dismiss him as automatically as she had other, less dynamic men.

He was older for one thing, in his early thirties. He was also very tall, well over six foot, with wide shoulders, narrow hips and long powerful legs. The rock-hard muscles of his arms, back and torso showed easily beneath the cotton cloth of his work shirts, and his hands were big, with calluses and scars few city men would have had.

Marla had watched him ride horses and deal with cattle, and there didn't seem to be anything he couldn't handle, whether it had to do with work or animals or people. She couldn't imagine him being afraid of anything, and she was certain no one ever trifled with him.

Except Jaicey. As hard and macho as he was, he was gentle and indulgent with his little sister. It was clear he adored her and had always been the ideal big brother.

He was a good son to his father, but also his father's equal in authority, though Jake deferred to him and showed him complete respect. The bond between father and son was as strong as steel, and along with Jaicey, they seemed the perfect family, even without the wife and mother they all kept in fond remembrance.

In truth, Marla had fallen a little in love with her sister's family and in spite of her best efforts, she yearned to be an open part of it. Jaicey had started her thinking about that when she'd pointed out that through her, Marla was kin to the Craddocks. Marla had quickly changed the subject before Jaicey could go on about it, but the seed of the notion had gone soul deep.

She needed to stop thinking about these things and calm down inside. The mysterious anxiety she felt was still growing. There was no real reason for it, so she needed to defeat it.

It didn't help to know that Jake could press the buzzer in the lobby any moment, so she paced the living room, hoping the activity would settle her nerves before he arrived.

In the end, it wasn't the buzzer in the lobby that alerted Marla to Jake's arrival. She'd just paced the length of the living room and turned to start back toward the sliding glass door to her small patio, when she saw the tall cowboy who waited on the other side of the glass.

CHAPTER TWO

MARLA FELT HER body go hot from scalp to toes as her brain registered the sight of Jake Craddock. The idea that Jaicey wanted this man to fall for her was more than a little terrifying. Yes, she was strongly attracted to him, but she wasn't sure she could survive if anything deep or truly emotional came of that attraction.

Emotions were dangerous at worst, unpredictable at best. She'd let Jaicey into her heart because she'd become convinced Jaicey was sincere, and that their blood kinship was no mirage.

The man at the door represented the worst kind of mirage, one of romantic love. She'd already learned a couple of painful lessons about falling in love, and she wasn't about to repeat them, no matter how strong the temptation.

The size of the man always made her feel small and ultrafeminine, never more than now as he stood framed by the patio door of her modest apartment. Before this she'd always seen him against the backdrop of the huge main house on Craddock Ranch or the range. He looked natural in those settings, but here he looked a little like a giant about to step into a child's playhouse.

He was dressed in a royal-blue shirt that fitted his hard body as if it had been specially tailored for him. Considering he could buy anything he liked, it probably had been. His jeans were a dark blue, and they encased his lean hips and powerful legs like a glove. His black boots were polished to a dull shine, and he wore a black dress Stetson.

Marla realized that she'd been staring like a fool, and managed to make her legs move again to walk to the slider. As she did she tried to give him a neutral smile. She'd been smiling fake smiles like this one for years, but tonight it felt strained.

Jake wasn't smiling, even to look polite, but that was no surprise. She noted again that his tanned face made him seem a good ten years too rugged and harsh for his age. But then, he spent the majority of his time outdoors, and she liked the squint lines that fanned out at the corners of his eyes and the long creases that bracketed the slash of his stern lips. He'd gotten them from smiling at someone, just not her.

He was no callow youth, but a seasoned male who seemed too worldly and experienced for her to ever feel completely at ease around. She was attracted to him anyway, deeply attracted, and that made her feel vaguely threatened. And cowardly. As she bent to roll the security bar out of the track and straightened to unlatch the door, she noticed that her fingers were trembling. She gave the glass panel a tug to slide it open, and finally allowed herself to fully meet his gaze.

His eyes were like black coals, and the banked glitter of fire in them showed for an instant before it disappeared. She'd almost missed it, but the relentless gleam of curiosity and cynicism lingered. There was no way to miss that.

She guessed he hadn't come here because his sister had persuaded him to. Though he probably did mean to apologize and invite her to the ranch, Marla suspected he wouldn't do either of those things because he wanted peace between them.

He'd come here tonight to say all the right words because it served his purpose. The other times she'd gone to the ranch, she'd been able to limit her contact with him. If she went camping this weekend, they'd be far from the usual distractions and he'd get a longer period of time to be around her. Would he be able to trip her up somehow? Catch some hint in an offhand remark?

Unless he'd already found out what he wanted to know. After all, it would be a simple thing to hire a private investigator. Once he found out details about her background, the rest wouldn't be hard to discover. If he hadn't told Jaicey what he'd found out, then it might be because he still suspected she was some kind of opportunist.

On the other hand, he probably hadn't hired an investigator. Jake Craddock seemed more the type to go after information on his own. He impressed her as the kind of man who enjoyed the challenge of a hunt, and the idea compelled her to find a way to shield herself.

It would be selfish to pressure Jaicey to confess their secret, at least to Jake, but she was sorely tempted to. She just wasn't up to walking on eggshells much longer, not when Jake looked at her like he was right now, like a hawk about to swoop down on small prey.

"Hello, Mr. Craddock," she said, forcing herself to sound pleasant and welcoming. "Won't you come in?"

She stepped back and waited until he'd crossed the threshold into her living room. Once he was inside he took off his Stetson, closed the slider for her, rolled the security bar into place, then stood glancing around.

"Would you like a soda? Coffee? It could be ready in no time."

He didn't answer as he looked around the room. Marla knew her apartment wasn't a fraction as grand as the Craddock home, but it was a tasteful, colorful collection of reconditioned furniture and interesting artwork, mostly bargains bought at auctions, estate sales and flea markets, if the price wasn't too high.

She tried again to get his attention. "Would you like to sit down?"

He turned toward her then. "I thought we could go for coffee somewhere. There's a pie house a few blocks over, if you're in the mood."

Marla felt her face flush. She hadn't expected this,

and dithered over what to say. The cynicism seemed to have evaporated from his eyes, and only a spark of male curiosity remained. He seemed for all the world like any other man who might ask her out for a cup of coffee. Her earlier impression of his motive for coming here tonight now seemed completely mistaken. Maybe he did want peace. Maybe he realized she wasn't scheming to take advantage of his sister.

Marla told herself it was for Jaicey's sake that she gave a small nod and said, "Yes, thank you, I think I'd like that," but that wasn't true. It was just better to see how he behaved while they were alone a short time before she committed herself to another weekend around him. And yet that wasn't quite true, either.

He responded to her answer with a slight curve of his stern lips, and Marla felt a flutter as the sexy charm of it struck. *That's* why she was going tonight, because of this sudden difference in him.

Her soft, "I just need to get my shoes and hand-bag…it shouldn't take long," gave her a reason to turn from that charm and seek temporary sanctuary in her bedroom down the hall while she tried to marshal both calm and sanity.

Jake Craddock was daunting enough as he usually was, but the Jake Craddock she'd just left in the living room could be lethal. The heat that had gone through her the moment she'd seen him had come roaring back when he'd smiled. She hadn't expected that, and from

here on she'd have to be on guard, more against the foolishness in herself than because of any intended threat
from him.

As she found the pair of loafers she wanted, Marla
discovered that the anxiety she'd felt earlier was mostly
gone. In its place was a wild combination of feminine
panic and excitement, which wasn't too much better
than the nameless anxiety. She had no idea why she'd
felt that earlier, but she knew why she felt what she did
now, and it meant real peril.

Maybe Jake would be a jerk at the pie house and
whatever it was that made her so susceptible to him
would be neutralized, or she'd finally see something
about him that made him seem a little more like an or-
dinary man she could easily forget about.

Disturbed that the idea made her heart sink, Marla
picked up her handbag and went back out to join him.

In her brief absence, Jake had chosen a seat at the end
of the sofa where he had room to stretch out his legs and
bypass the coffee table. Though the sofa was the larg-
est piece of furniture in the room, his size dominated it.
He'd upended his Stetson on the coffee table, and picked
up a throw pillow. It was one of two velvet crazy quilt
pillows that she'd cut and pieced herself from the bag
of fabric remnants she'd collected.

Jake was running the knuckles of one hand over the
rich textures as if he enjoyed them, before he stopped
to inspect the satiny stitch patterns that decorated the

seams. He seemed absorbed, almost fascinated, and Marla felt another flutter over how sensual his big fingers looked as they moved lightly over the stitching on the lush fabric.

"Did you make this yourself?" he asked without looking up.

Marla felt a small rush of delight over his interest, but she was embarrassed that he'd known she was quietly watching him. And was this harmless question the prelude for other, less harmless ones? In spite of Jaicey's assurances, the idea put her on guard again.

"I do some quilting," she said quietly. He looked at her, his gaze lit with interest.

"You're good at it. Damned good."

Her soft, "Thank you," was accompanied by the uneasy drop of her gaze. She wasn't comfortable with the warm pleasure his compliment gave her. She didn't trust it, either. What could a cowboy know about quilting or the quality of needlework?

"I'm ready to leave whenever you are," she said, trying to reclaim her common sense.

Jake set the pillow aside and came to his feet, "I've got something to say before we go."

The tension in her middle pulled tight. "Oh?"

Marla had to keep from biting her lip over that one. She shouldn't pretend she didn't know he was about to apologize, but she suddenly hoped he'd skip it. For one thing, he hadn't been mean to her or disrespectful when he'd asked his questions. Second—and most important—it would be better for her foolish heart if he didn't apologize. She suddenly needed that extra barrier between them.

"I reckon you know how much I think of my sister," he began, and Marla made herself look at him. His expression was solemn and his dark gaze was fastened on hers as if he was trying to read her mind.

"Jaicey's got about a million friends," he said, "but none like you, a stranger one day and a close friend the next."

His gaze pressed deeper into hers, as if he was looking for one last hint that would confirm his suspicion and spare him from apologizing. "But Jaicey vouched for your good character, so...I apologize for prying."

Marla knew right away that Jaicey's endorsement wasn't quite enough for Jake, but she decided to pretend it was. She was acutely aware of the enormity of what she and Jaicey were keeping from him, and his apology made her feel guilty.

"Thank you. I can't blame you for wanting to look out for Jaicey." Her guilt sharpened, so she abruptly changed the subject. To her private horror, haste made her babble.

"We might as well take separate cars. I need to dash to the market later to pick up a couple of things, so I can spare you a trip back here."

That sounded lame, and now Jake's steady gaze was

sending little earthquakes of dismay through her that were powerfully disruptive. Could he tell how guilty she felt? How guilty she *was?* One side of his handsome mouth kicked up in another sexy smile.

"It's only a few blocks, Miss Marlie," he said, his low drawl going softer. "I can take you shopping afterward, and bring you home after that."

Her nerves all but twanged over that, but she tried to smile and not let it look like a twitch. "All right."

Jake bent to pick up his Stetson from the coffee table before he moved closer. "I thought you and I could make a fresh start tonight."

His low voice had gone smoky, and she wasn't such a novice that she didn't know when a man was about to make a romantic move of some sort.

"That might be nice," she said, then wished she'd thought of something less encouraging to say.

Flustered, she turned to walk toward the hall door. She could feel Jake's dark gaze wander over her back, and his nearness made her skin tingle, particularly when they reached the hall and Jake took her elbow to escort her to the lobby.

It was just a casual touch, but it felt anything but casual to her. There was a prickly energy that flowed between them, some primitive message from male to female that made her heart race and her body go a little weak.

She was in over her head with a man like Jake. He

was too dynamic, too sexy, too macho, and he made her feel things no man had ever made her feel. They had nothing in common but Jaicey, and he was light years more experienced sexually than she believed she'd ever be.

He was the kind of man who brought all kinds of emotional disruptions, but also the worst kind of heartache once the initial chemistry fizzled out. She'd seen that happen to others, and she'd rather be single for the rest of her life than get herself in that kind of emotional mess.

Whatever naïve notions Jaicey had, a man as worldly and experienced and rich as Jake was would never think of someone like her as a serious romantic possibility, and she needed to be careful. There was nothing worse than pining for a man you could neither have nor cope with if you could have him. Jake Craddock certainly fit both descriptions.

It seemed to take forever to get out of the building and walk to his pickup across the street. At last he opened the passenger door and supported her elbow for the climb up. After he released her and stepped back to close the door, she breathed a quiet sigh of relief.

Marla had never ridden in a pickup before coming to Texas, and she'd liked them right away. She tried to focus on the truck as Jake walked around to the driver's side. Her economy car was small and closer to the ground, so she liked the novelty of the size and the engine power of the big vehicle. She also loved the high profile. It made her feel safer, and she could see so much more from here than in her car.

The other advantage of the big pickup was that there was more space between them than in a regular car. Since Jake was a little overwhelming, she appreciated that small distance. Maybe she'd get used to him soon, and she wouldn't be so aware of his every move. Or remember so clearly how her body had reacted to his touch.

Time with Jake did nothing to diminish that awareness. If anything, she became more sensitized to him. He was the perfect gentleman the whole time, telling her things about the history of Coulter City and the area, mentioning places she ought to see, then offering to show her around weekend after next. Because she was so taken by this mellow and engaging side of Jake, Marla barely paid attention to the excellent flavor of the pecan pie slice she'd ordered. It was almost a surprise when the waitress came back to whisk away their empty plates.

As they sat across from each other in a booth at the pie house with a coffee refill, Jake officially invited her to come to the ranch that weekend.

"I've never gone camping," Marla told him. "Do you use tents?"

She wasn't sure she was ready to sleep on the open ground like Jaicey had told her they often did during roundup. In truth, she shouldn't even think about going to the ranch, but Jake's new attitude toward her was very persuasive.

"My father and I usually don't, but you and Jaicey will have a tent. A couple of cots if you want them. Jaicey cooks over the campfire. It's about the only time she likes to cook."

"What do you do besides sleep under the stars and cook over a fire?" she asked, but his answer was interrupted by the ring of his cell phone.

Marla looked down into her coffee as he took the call, automatically wanting to give him what privacy she could. She sensed the tension in him almost right away, and glanced at his face.

His stony expression was unreadable beyond the fact that it was grave. Shock had widened his eyes, and it was that sign of vulnerability that gave her a stab of dread. And then he practically erupted out of the booth, digging in a pocket for money as he rapped out a curt, "I'll be right there."

Marla had reached for her handbag and slid to the edge of the booth seat to stand as she responded to the urgency in him. Jake tossed a bill on the table and shoved the phone into his jeans' pocket.

"Family emergency. I need to take you home."

Marla felt a leap of panic. "Then you go on. I'll get myself home."

"Just let me take you," he said tersely, and took her arm to stalk to the door.

Marla had to almost run to keep up with his long stride. By the time they got to his truck and she climbed in, she was almost wild to know if the family emergency was because of Judd or Jaicey. It was terrible to hope it was Judd, but she couldn't seem to help herself.

Jake started the truck engine and checked traffic before he pulled away from the curb.

"Is it your father?" she asked once he began to accelerate.

An impatient shake of his head made her dread shoot to raw fear. "It's Jaicey. A car crash."

Marla's head swam and she lifted a hand to her temple, as if that small act could steady her. Her adoptive father had been killed in a wreck. It had been the beginning of the end for her little family.

"Did they say how bad it was?" she ventured, knowing already what the answer was. Jake's voice lowered to a growl.

"Bad."

Her heart dropped and her brain wouldn't function for moments more as she struggled not to faint.

CHAPTER THREE

MARLA finally faced forward, dazed. Pain and an old feeling of futility and loss swept through her. The sudden slowing of the pickup made her realize they were about to turn onto her street, and her impulse was to tell Jake to drive on.

"You don't have to take me home," she got out. "Please, just go straight to the hospital."

"I don't want to worry about you getting home." The gruff sound of his voice emphasized his refusal, and Marla felt herself recoil with hurt. She shouldn't have said anything about going on. Jake was obviously shaken, and she'd only been thinking of herself. Of course he wouldn't want an outsider around at a time like this.

Sick with remorse, Marla tried to cope with the misery and terror if being left off at home while Jaicey's life was at risk. She couldn't even follow in her own car now. Jake's refusal to take her with him, though they both knew she could catch a cab later, was a not-so-subtle message that he didn't want her there at all.

Of course he wouldn't. He and his father barely knew her, and she was ashamed that it must have looked like she meant to barge in. Perhaps it was also a confirmation of her sense that in spite of Jake's apology and the pleasant hour or so they'd spent together tonight, he still disapproved of Jaicey's friendship with her.

She'd almost started to believe tonight had been genuine, when she of all people shouldn't have let herself be taken in.

Jaicey could be dying...

The agony of thinking that dominated every other thought, and the sick knot in her middle wouldn't relent. The only relief she got was when Jake pulled the pickup to a jarring halt at the front walk of her apartment building. She was out in a flash. She'd meant to rush to the front door, but she felt too unsteady.

The knot in her middle was growing at an alarming rate, making her legs and arms feel weak. Nausea swamped her, and she barely made it past her apartment door before dizziness hit so hard she barely made it down the hall to the bathroom. She spent that next hour sitting on the closed commode, bathing her face and neck with cold water, praying like she'd never prayed in her life.

If it were possible to trade her life for Jaicey's, she'd do it in a heartbeat, and told God as much. It wasn't fair for beautiful, full of life Jaicey to be badly hurt or to be in danger of dying so young. Her life mattered to so many people, especially her family. Jaicey had so much to live for, so much yet to do, so many years ahead of her.

It was wrong for Jaicey to be at risk, so wrong, especially when Marla sat uselessly in her bathroom trying to stave off a breakdown and not choke on the guilt of being healthy and whole and safe while her sister could very well be fighting for her life.

She had no one but Jaicey, no grand plans for the future, no important impact to make on the world. Not like Jaicey. If it had to happen to one of them, why hadn't it been her?

Please, God...

And what about Judd? He must be out of his mind over this. Jaicey had worried so much about confessing their secret, but the accident had to be a million times worse for him than some paltry confession.

Marla had a thought that maybe Jaicey hadn't been hurt as badly as Jake had initially believed. Perhaps once he'd gotten to the hospital, he'd found out that Jaicey's injuries were minor. Her heart failed to rally over that idea, and she again thought about Judd.

Please God, he's such a nice old man.

Eventually Marla recovered enough to make her way back out into the living room to sit on the sofa. Compelled to seek information, she switched on the TV remote and clicked through the channels, stopping on one for twenty-four hour news that featured a rebroadcast of weather and news highlights from one of her local stations. She managed to catch a repeat of the local segment just as it was coming on. The news anchor was unusually solemn and melodramatic.

"A deadly accident takes three lives, leaving another in the balance."

Marla's heart crowded into her throat. Video of a freeway exit ramp at a Coulter City intersection she didn't recognize showed a stopped semitrailer truck with two passenger cars smashed together behind it.

According to witnesses, the semi had stopped at the traffic light, as had the car behind it. A second car exiting the freeway had barreled into the back of the first car, shoving it into the back of the truck's huge trailer. The high-speed impact had been violent enough to crush the first car and crumple the front end of the second like an accordion.

It was hard to tell if either of the late-model cars were Jaicey's, because both were dark and mangled. How could anyone in either car have survived?

Marla didn't realize she'd grabbed one of the velvet crazy quilt pillows to clutch to her chest. She was unable to look away from the TV screen, or to even breathe until the news piece was ending.

"The names of the victims have not been released pending notification of the families…A tragic, tragic night in Coulter City…"

Grief pushed down on her, and she felt her insides shrivel under the sick weight. She tried to convince herself that this wasn't the wreck Jaicey had been in, but her heart thudded heavily with the strange knowledge that it was. The idea that Jaicey had been somewhere in that tangle of metal was more than she could stand.

And if seeing a video of the wreck was this hard on her, what about Jake and Judd? Her eyes burned and her throat was dry and prickly. She was suffocating with grief, but there was nothing she could do to relieve it. She was too shocked to cry.

I feel like there's no time…

Jaicey had said that. They'd both felt it, almost from the day they'd met face-to-face. The unbearable weight of grief settled in deeper, and Marla began to tremble.

His father's face was ashen beneath his tan. Jake kept a close watch over him as they sat in the surgical waiting room. Connie Lane was there, too. Phoning the retired nurse to come sit with them eased some of his concern about how his father was taking this. Connie was a veteran of both family emergencies and hard times, and there was no one better able to be a calming influence on his father.

Jaicey was still in the operating room and if she held on, she'd be in surgery most of the night. She had a head injury, internal bleeding, broken bones and a collapsed lung. She'd lost a lot of blood, but Connie had reminded them that Jaicey was young and vital, and that she was too strong not to fight for her life. He prayed that was so.

Earlier, before his father had seen, Jake had managed to intercept the deputy who'd come to the surgical floor to speak to them. They'd gone to an empty waiting room on another floor to discuss the wreck.

According to the officer, a car of drunks had been joyriding on the freeway. The deputy had just pulled on to give chase, but he'd no more than spotted the taillights ahead when the speeding car crossed four lanes and hurtled off the exit.

The crash happened in the seconds before the squad car reached the exit, so all the officer had been able to do was call fire rescue and an ambulance. Another sheriff's deputy had closed the exit ramp to traffic while firemen used the "jaws of life" to free Jaicey from her car.

"She's lucky to be alive," the deputy had said. The three young men in the other car had either died on impact or soon after.

Once the deputy had handed over a card with the case number of the wreck and gone out, Jake had stayed a while in the empty waiting room. He'd switched on the nearby TV in time to see the late news.

As the deputy had told him, a film crew had gotten to the scene just after the rescue crew had arrived, but the news video had only shown the aftermath of the rescue. Jaicey's car had been smashed against—and partway underneath—the back of the semitrailer. That she'd survived in one piece was a miracle. Now she needed another miracle, maybe a lot of them...

It had been hours now since Jake had come back to join his father and Miss Connie in the waiting room. Jake glanced at Judd then at the wall clock opposite the small grouping of chairs and a sofa: 4:00 a.m.

Helplessness churned in his gut, but the desolation in his heart was unlike anything he'd ever felt in his life. Restless, he got up to head to the nurses' station for an update. He knew he'd get some kind of patient, neutral answer, perhaps hear a professionally soothing, "Sorry," but he needed to do something.

He waited to walk away until Connie made eye contact with him. She seemed able to read his mind and gave him a subtle nod as she absently rubbed Judd's shoulder in silent reassurance. Judd was staring at nothing, the hollowness about him aging him a good twenty years. The tall strong man who'd always, even in illness, been rawhide tough and damned near invincible, suddenly looked washed out and dangerously weak.

The daughter who'd been the joy of his life was barely hanging on, with a long road to recovery even if she survived. Jake knew like he knew the sun would come up in the next hour or so that his father would never get over it if they lost Jaicey.

His feeling of helplessness mounted, goading him to do something, to act. The frustration of being unable to do anything worth a damn dogged him as he walked to the nurse's station. He had a brief flash of Marla's stricken face when he'd said the words "family emergency," but after that he didn't give her another thought.

The only sleep Marla got came after 5:30 a.m., but according to the antique wooden clock she'd restored, a mere twenty minutes had gone by since she'd drifted off.

Still feeling foggy, she rose from the sofa, chafing her arms to get warm. She should have turned down the air-conditioning hours ago. She should have slept under a quilt from the linen closet or gone to bed.

She should have heard something about Jaicey by now.

Her tired brain kept circling back to her sister. Had Jaicey been strong enough to have surgery if she'd needed it? Or had it been too late to save her? Was she gone, or had she survived the night? Was it even remotely possible, as she'd hoped last night, that Jake had gotten to the hospital and found that Jaicey wasn't as badly hurt as the doctors had originally thought?

Marla probably wouldn't be on his call list, no matter how things had turned out with Jaicey. As she'd seen at the end last night, Jake was anything but okay with her being around his family, no matter how nice he'd tried to be before he'd gotten the call.

Perhaps her perception of his attitude was wrong, though she didn't think so. Maybe when Jake Craddock had a shock, he didn't deal well with people on the periphery. Maybe he couldn't handle everything, as she'd thought. On the other hand, he'd just been talking to her about spending the weekend at the ranch with his family as if he'd accepted her as a family friend.

It didn't take much to know that if she'd been any other friend of Jaicey's—a friend he approved of—he might have found time to give her a quick call, or had someone else call to fill her in. It hurt to realize that, but Marla couldn't bring herself to think badly of him for it. He had no idea who she was to Jaicey, no idea at all, and apparently the differences in her and her sister were strong enough that he might never suspect.

Marla forced herself through a shower and mechanically took care of drying her hair, brushing her teeth and putting on a little makeup. She chose a cheery pink blouse for luck, and a black skirt with small pink blooms that complemented the blouse, then slid her feet into a pair of heels, got her handbag and started for work.

It was her day to pick up the bakery box for the office, so she stopped at the market, adding a carton of real cream and another of chocolate milk for an extra Friday morning treat before she drove on to work. She delivered her packages to the break room, paged through the morning newspaper and read every word of the brief article about the wreck. Jaicey was identified by name, but there was no word on her condition. The paper must have gotten only a bit of info before the Friday issue had gone to press.

Marla struggled to believe Jaicey hadn't died, and it

was a trial to concentrate on her work and to behave normally. She had no idea if she accomplished either, but no one commented so she must have done well enough.

It was all she could do not to call Craddock Ranch and ask about Jaicey, but she was at work and she was too new to the job to leave early if she got bad news. Of course, it would be different if she could tell her employers that she and Jaicey were sisters. Marla couldn't breathe a word of that, so she was forced to wait until 5:00 p.m. to leave.

The tedium of the slow-passing hours made the wait unbearable and interfered so much with her concentration that she worked through lunch and ended up leaving the office at half past six.

At last she was driving home, using the hope of a call on her answering machine to stay alert. A strong fatigue was settling over her, a reminder of how little sleep she'd gotten last night. By the time she got to a parking space at the apartment building, she felt drugged.

Miserable with it and the worry that had kept her in knots all day, Marla got out of her car and doggedly walked to the building's back door. Movement seemed to revive her a little, but when she got into her apartment and went to her answering machine in the bedroom, there was no message waiting for her, so she tapped in the number for Craddock Ranch.

The first two times, her call went right into the ranch's voice mail system before a third was picked up by the housekeeper, Miss Jenny. The woman's calm drawl was as steady and unruffled as usual, and it eased some of Marla's upset.

"Hello, Miss Jenny," she rushed out, "this is Marla Norris. I was with Mr. Craddock when he got the news about the accident, but I haven't heard anything today about how Jaicey is." Her dread shot to dry-mouthed terror, and she braced for the answer.

"Jaicey made it through surgery last night and this morning," the woman answered quickly as if to spare Marla the distress of a wait, "and was holdin' on last I heard. The doc says the next forty-eight hours'll tell. I'm sorry I didn't get you called yet, but the phone's been ringin' all day, and it wasn't something I wanted to leave on your answering machine."

Marla's knees gave out and she dropped to the edge of the bed, relieved to hear Jaicey was alive but terrified by the news that her sister's survival was so uncertain.

"It's…that bad?" Saying the words made her nauseous. Miss Jenny's voice went lower.

"Pretty bad, honey," she said, "but we're not givin' up on her. Mr. Jake and Mr. Judd are either at the hospital or stayin' in town so they'll be close. I expect I'll hear something more from one of them tonight. In the meantime, there's nothing the rest of us can do that's worth much, except pray. Good thing prayin's the best thing you can do."

Marla wasn't as confident of that as Jenny seemed

to be, but her skepticism made her feel tremendous guilt, as if she might somehow spoil Jaicey's chances if she didn't put faith in prayer.

Whether to defy her doubt and convince herself, or to perhaps convince God that she was willing to believe in prayer, Marla gave a soft, "Yes, that is the best thing" before Jenny went on.

"Well, I 'spect there's gonna be more calls comin' in—like I said, they have been all day—so it's best I don't talk too long. I'll be sure to give you a call whenever I hear somethin' more. That okay with you?"

"That's fine with me, Miss Jenny, thanks. And you can call me anytime, no matter how late," she said, then added, "or early," because she wanted to be sure the woman understood she meant tomorrow morning, too, if need be. A moment later they told each other good-bye and Marla hung up.

Marla slipped off her shoes and sat there a while, her arms wrapped around herself for comfort. At least Jaicey was still alive, and as long as she was alive there was hope. Marla made herself get up and go to the kitchen to find something to eat, but the sandwich she fixed was impossible to finish. Still dressed for work, she went to the living room and picked up the TV remote to switch on the news before she got ready for an early bedtime.

She should have gone straight to the shower. Instead she sat down briefly in the armchair. The soft cushions drew her deeper into the chair, and she felt her body relax. She'd expected a quick meal to give her a second wind, but she'd no more than remembered that before her lashes dropped closed and the newscast ebbed to a low drone.

Jake wasn't interested in anything more demanding than driving around Coulter City with his pickup windows down. He'd spent most of the past twenty-four hours at the hospital. So had his father. Connie had finally convinced Judd to sleep in a bed that night, but he'd refused to leave the hospital unless Jake did the same, so they'd all gone to her house.

Jake had taken a quick shower there, and put on some fresh clothes from the suitcase Miss Jenny had sent to town for him, but he hadn't been able to sit around Connie's house. He couldn't bring himself to drive out to the ranch because it was too far from the hospital, and he'd been cooped up too long in waiting rooms to tolerate being indoors just yet.

The fresh night air streaming in the pickup windows was sultry, but it didn't do much to lift his preoccupation with Jaicey. Sweet little Jaicey, so battered and broken and hurt. Still holding on, though, and that gave him hope.

It was after eleven before he realized which street he'd turned onto a few blocks ago. As if his pickup had a mind of its own, it slowed then pulled into the driveway of Marla Norris's apartment building to coast around to the parking lot behind.

His gaze automatically picked out her patio door. The drapes were wide-open, and her TV was on. Jake slowed the truck to a stop and felt a needle of disapproval when he saw that she was sitting in the armchair that practically faced the glass. Any man walking past could look his fill, particularly at the enticing legs that were illuminated by the light from the TV screen. Didn't girls from the big city protect their privacy better than that?

He knew it was irrational to be irritated with her, but he couldn't seem to help it. And he felt guilty. Whatever he thought about her friendship with Jaicey, he should have phoned her that day. Marla seemed to have genuine feelings of friendship for his sister—Jaicey certainly thought so—but none of them really knew much about her.

He didn't buy that she'd moved from Chicago to a small town in Texas to be closer to family. He had yet to hear about a single family member who'd come to Coulter City to visit, and he was fairly certain she hadn't visited any. None of the Norrises in town knew her, and Jaicey had been as vague about where her family lived as Marla was. Could she be running from something up north? Some*one?* And on practically the day she'd moved to town, she'd taken up with Jaicey.

Marla Norris was too guarded, and she didn't like questions. She wasn't a good liar, either, and the patchy color that came into her cheeks told him she was not only ashamed of the vague and probably untrue answers she gave, but that she also had a lot to hide. Which was why he figured she was running from something.

So why the hell had he come here? Why was he staring at her like this so late at night? It was almost as if he was looking for a reason to park his truck and go knock on her door. Aggravated by that he drove away, following the exit driveway around to the front of the apartment building before he turned onto the street. He'd meant to drive on, to forget about Marla Norris, but for some reason his brain refused to acknowledge, he pulled his truck into an open parking space.

CHAPTER FOUR

THE harsh ring woke her up, and Marla grabbed blindly for the telephone. It took a second or two to dawn on her that she was hearing a dial tone instead of a voice. The lobby buzzer sounded, making her realize it must have awakened her instead of the phone. As she hung up the receiver, she glanced at the clock to see the time. Eleven-twenty. A third short buzz brought her up out of the chair to go to the call box next to the hall door.

"Yes?"

A rough, masculine voice answered. "Jake Craddock. Is it too late to come in?"

Marla's heart leaped with surprise and pleasure before it fell back into dread. Why would Jake come here at this time of night? The fear for Jaicey that had been blessedly absent just now spiraled up.

"No, it's not too late," she said hastily, then pressed the button that would briefly unlock the lobby door.

After a few more tense seconds, Marla realized she

was too anxious to wait for Jake's knock. She opened the door and looked down the hall just as he came into sight. She tried to read his solemn features for any hint of Jaicey's condition, but saw little more than weariness at first. The big, tough Texan looked a little beaten down, and that got her by the heart.

As he strode closer, she began to read frightening things in the bleakness in his eyes. He looked grim and a little spooked, and that unnerved her. She couldn't wait another moment for news.

"Jaicey—is she going to be all right?"

Jake gently took her arm and turned her to walk into the apartment. The gesture conveyed the human need to connect with another, suggesting an almost confidential closeness between good friends that went straight to her marrow.

"She's stable."

"Oh, thank God," Marla said. "When I saw your face just now—" She cut herself off.

Unbelievably rattled by the impression of closeness and Jake's warm, hard fingers around her upper arm, Marla pulled away and took a safe step back as he closed the door and reached up to pull off his Stetson. Even without the hat, he towered over her, and she could feel the steadiness and natural protectiveness in his character. The sense of safety he radiated tonight wrapped around her like a warm fist, and it was a struggle to bring her thoughts back to Jaicey's condition. The effort it took appalled her, and that prompted second thoughts about what Jake had meant when he'd said Jaicey was stable.

"Stable…that's good, isn't it?"

"Better," he allowed as he tiredly upended his Stetson on the small entry table.

"Was the wreck on TV last night the one she was in?"

"'Fraid so."

"What are her injuries? Concussion? Broken bones?"

Now that she could actually speak to someone who'd been there to hear what the doctors had said and had seen Jaicey's condition for himself, Marla couldn't keep from pestering him for details. It never entered her mind to invite him to step into the living room and sit down. News about Jaicey was more important than manners.

"Those, plus internal injuries. The biggest worry is the head injury."

"You've seen her?" Marla persisted anxiously. "Is she awake?"

Jake gave his head a slight shake and ran a weary hand through his dark, overlong hair in what was no doubt a subconscious indication of how deeply worried he was.

"I've seen her," he said somberly as his gaze avoided direct contact with hers. "She could be out of it for days, maybe weeks. It'll take her months to get well, if—"

He was weary enough not to completely catch himself before he'd started to say the words "if she lives," but Marla heard them as clearly as if he had. Dread swelled in her heart.

"But she's *stable*," Marla burst out in a sudden need to deny the foreboding she felt. She didn't realize she'd taken firm hold of his forearm to emphasize the word until the heat of his skin registered on her palm and fingers and penetrated her fear.

His big hand came up and caught hers, not just to remove it from his arm but to give her fingers a squeeze of agreement.

"That's right," he growled as if he'd taken a cue from the determination in the way she'd said it. "She's stable." Now his dark eyes fully connected with hers and strong will glittered in their depths, as if he meant to dictate Jaicey's recovery. "She's strong and stubborn. She loves life too much to quit it now."

Marla's heart stirred forcefully, buoyed by the steely certainty in his low voice. "And life loves her. She can't leave now, not until she's at least ninety years old."

"Make that a hundred."

The current of will and wish was suddenly infused by strong emotion, and their grip on each other's fingers tightened. The hope they'd tried to summon to quell feelings of anguish and fear intensified that strong emotion.

Marla couldn't begin to name what she was feeling—wouldn't *dare* put a name to it—but she somehow sensed Jake was feeling it too. The notion made her weak-kneed, completely unable to either look away from his rugged face or to let go of his hand. It was as if he could see into her heart through her eyes, and though she felt helplessly exposed, she couldn't make herself stop him for several skipping heartbeats of time.

Finally she was able to break contact with his gaze, but when she tried to pull her hand from his, he gave her a tug that brought her so close they were little more than a hand span from full contact. His other hand settled warmly on her waist to keep her there.

The air suddenly went heavy and it was hard to get in a full breath. The heat pouring off Jake's big body penetrated her clothes and her skin tingled. Something sweet and hot began to stir inside her, and as she looked up at him she felt a delicious quiver that she interpreted as a sensual awakening.

Exhaustion and the late hour combined to give the moment a dreamy unreality that began to set off little alarms and brought sanity back with a jolt. The look in Jake's dark eyes was fiery and intense, and she couldn't mistake the harsh desire on his rugged face. Had they both lost their minds? Or was she so tired she was dreaming after all?

Marla abruptly pulled away, horrified at how suddenly it had happened, and while Jaicey was so hurt and her future so threatened. Some sister she was!

"I'm tired," she got out, feeling stupid. "I think I was on the verge of falling asleep. Sorry."

It was an idiotic thing to say and a complete lie. On the other hand, maybe it wasn't a lie. She still doubted she was Jake Craddock's favorite person so perhaps she had imagined the past few moments. At the very least she had to have misinterpreted the whole thing, and her face went hot with embarrassment. It would be smart to thank him for bringing news and to send him on his way as quickly as possible.

"I'll bet you're worn out, too," she babbled on, "so I won't keep you any longer. It was good of you to stop by to update me about Jaicey. I really appreciate it."

For one of the rare times she'd seen it, Jake's handsome mouth curved a little.

"'Here's your hat, what's your hurry,'" he said, quoting an old expression that depicted the rush to get an unwanted guest out the door. Marla felt her face go doubly hot. His voice lowered to a rasp.

"But you're right. This isn't the time."

He released her to reach for his Stetson while she reeled with comprehension and then disbelief. This wasn't the time...for *what?*

He opened her apartment door and gave her a last look, his expression solemn again. "Don't forget to close your drapes after dark," he said. "No tellin' who might look in at you and get ideas."

A faint look of surprise crossed his face, followed instantly by a disgruntled frown.

"Just shut the damned drapes," he added gruffly before he turned to walk out, leaving her with a new shock as the door closed behind him.

Marla felt as if she'd lost her grip on the English language, or that the meaning of common words suddenly didn't quite fit their intended message.

She tried to make sense of the past moments as she closed the drapes and switched off the television. It surprised her a little to realize the TV had been droning on at a low volume the whole time Jake had been here, and she felt even more unsettled. Once he'd walked in, he'd stolen her awareness of everything but news of Jaicey and those charged minutes by the door.

At least Jaicey was holding on. Marla tried to take encouragement from that, especially since Jaicey must be close to midway through the forty-eight hours Miss Jenny had mentioned. Apparently she was doing well enough that Jake could take time to drop by and tell her about it in person.

Relieved but too tired now to bother with a shower, Marla dressed for bed and put out the light. Sleep delayed long enough for her brain to review every word, every look and every impression of Jake's brief visit as she tried to see meanings that made sense.

Her initial conclusion—that she'd seen and interpreted every moment just as it had happened, and that Jake Craddock was attracted to *her*—made her deeply uncomfortable. She fell asleep before she could construct an alternate conclusion she could ignore, or at least live peaceably with.

* * *

The next day was Saturday, but Marla woke up only a few minutes later than on workdays. She'd slept hard and felt reasonably rested before a feeling of restlessness began to nettle her. She did her usual Saturday chores, started some laundry in the compact washer in one end of her bathroom, then checked her grocery list and got ready to go out.

Though she was reluctant to leave the apartment, she did it anyway. Miss Jenny had promised to keep her updated and since there'd been no call, it must mean that nothing much had changed with Jaicey.

Getting out lifted her spirits a little, and being around other shoppers in the market helped give the day a better feeling of normalcy. She tried to cling to that feeling of normalcy as the hours stretched. She heard briefly from Miss Jenny after lunch. Jaicey had shown slight improvement, and Marla felt some of her restlessness ease.

After she'd started another load of laundry, she went into her spare bedroom that served as a sewing room, to work on the quilt top she'd been piecing. She only had a fourth of it to go. Once she lightly pressed the seams, she could move some of the furniture around in the living room and lay out the quilt back, batting and quilt top so she could carefully baste the layers together. When she finished that, she could secure it in a quilting hoop and begin hand stitching.

Working with the fabric pieces was relaxing and satisfying, but it was work that didn't require much thought. Time and again she found herself thinking about last night, mentally reliving everything Jake had said and done.

What was wrong with her? She'd never been this affected by a man before, never brooded over one like this, not even the two she'd fallen for. She'd daydreamed about getting married, having a home and raising a family, but now she realized that she'd been more enthralled by the idea of belonging and having a family than she'd been with the young men she'd hoped to have them with.

It was almost the reverse with Jake Craddock. She was overwhelmed by thoughts of the man. Yes, she craved the security he represented, but security wasn't what she thought about when she remembered the way she'd felt when he touched her.

Even now, remembering the warm sensation of the hard calluses across his palms and fingers gave her a shiver. The firm but loose grip he'd had on her waist as he'd held her was unforgettable, but the memory of his nearness sent a flush through her. She might never forget the way his dark eyes had burned down at her, man to woman, as if...

Curiosity about the hard curve of Jake's mouth and how it might feel on hers filled her mind. It was several minutes before she realized she'd stopped pressing the foot pedal of the sewing machine, and that she'd been staring blindly down at the needle tip poised over the narrow seam.

The foolishness of her thoughts was jarring, and she impatiently finished the seam then briskly removed it from the machine. Once she knotted the threads and trimmed the excess, she switched off the tiny guide light and slid back her chair to stand. She'd been lost in a romantic daydream that had no hope of ever coming true, not even if she went against every shred of common sense she had and tried to make it come true. Why couldn't she get that through her head?

Now the restlessness was back, and she left the room to check on her laundry before she looked around the apartment for a task that would help her focus on something more productive.

Jaicey made it past the forty-eight hour time frame, and over those next several days she slowly began to improve. Miss Jenny was wonderfully faithful about keeping Marla updated. Meanwhile, she'd heard nothing from Jake directly and convinced herself it was for the best.

Jaicey was still in Intensive Care, but she was awake for small periods of time. Marla longed to go see her, but only family was allowed in the ICU and this wasn't the time to let the Craddocks know she was family.

It was just as well. Jaicey was in a fight to survive and get better, and Marla didn't want her to be distracted from that or to waste precious energy on her, no matter how much Marla wanted to see her.

As those first days passed and Miss Jenny's updates

continued to be positive, Marla was able to relax a bit, though the hours still seemed to drag. She welcomed going to work and once she wasn't on the razor's edge of anxiety and suspense, she was able to concentrate and achieve her usual level of productivity.

At home she spent a lot of time on the quilt. When that became too tedious, she began to go for long walks after work. Though the worst heat of the day had passed by evening, it was still hot, though she was adjusting to it. Once she had a shower and a light supper, she was better able to settle in to do needlework and the restlessness that had been plaguing her finally settled completely. The worst part was how much she missed Jaicey, and there was no distraction strong enough to defeat the ache of that.

The days stretched into a week, then two, and at last Miss Jenny reported that Jaicey had been moved from the ICU to a private room and could now have visitors.

"Course, she won't be up to more'n a few minutes at a time, but I'm sure she'd love to see you," Miss Jenny assured her that Saturday afternoon, just over two weeks after the wreck. "Mr. Judd's with her all day so Mr. Jake can work, then Mr. Jake goes to spell him in the evening. At least they're both back to sleepin' at home now that the worst is over."

The moment Marla thanked her and said goodbye, she hung up and excitedly dialed a local florist to send flowers. Since it was late Saturday afternoon she almost missed getting the order in before the last hospital delivery of the day. After that, she went to the sewing room to find the velvet teddy bear she'd made a couple of years ago.

The bear's crazy quilt pattern was a lot like the throw pillows on the sofa, but these velvet pieces were tiny and ultra soft with jewel-like colors. Since the fabric bits had been so small, she'd pieced them together by hand. She'd used a delicate rose satin for the face, paw pads and inside ears, including a tiny, heart-shaped red velvet patch on the bear's chest.

She'd filled it with a very squeezable stuffing, but the arms and legs were a bit narrower and longer than usual. Originally Marla had designed them differently to give infant hands an easier way to hold onto them. She'd meant to make a few to give for baby showers, but she'd been lured to other quilt projects and decided to keep the bear in hope of one day giving it to her own baby.

That possibility now seemed far away, so the bear would make a nice get well gift. Jaicey loved stuffed animals and still kept a few of them in her bedroom with a few more scattered around the Craddock house for visiting children to play with.

It was a whimsical gift, but the moment she decided to give it to Jaicey, it became a very emotional one. She held the plush bear to her cheek for a few moments in an almost childish need for contact.

"Remind her how much I love her," she whispered, then eased the bear away. The bear's wooden eyes seemed to twinkle, but it was the sheen of tears in Marla's own eyes that had caused it. She'd managed to keep the worry and longing and fear of the past two weeks from overwhelming her, but the dam of reserve that had held it back felt weak suddenly.

Marla determinedly pushed her emotions aside as she carried the bear to her bedroom. Once she changed clothes, she could start for the hospital.

When she reached the floor Jaicey was on and found her room, Marla begin to have second thoughts about the timing of her visit. Was Jaicey awake? Was she truly up to having visitors?

Something much worse occurred to her then. How did Jaicey look? Miss Jenny had warned that her beautiful golden hair had been partly shaved, and that her face still had a lot of swelling and discoloration. Jaicey had also suffered some facial cuts, but Marla had no idea how bad they were. Not for anything did she want to upset her sister by showing a reaction of surprise or shock or even too much sympathy, so she paused a moment outside the door to prepare herself.

It didn't matter to Marla what Jaicey looked like, but it would surely matter to Jaicey. They both were a bit vain about their looks, but Jaicey was truly gorgeous so it might be hard on her if she didn't look her beautiful best just yet. On the other hand, she couldn't be in any condition to fret over something so trivial.

Marla suddenly couldn't wait another moment to see her sister and pushed hesitantly against the partially closed door to peek around the edge.

Jake sat in the room chair she could see, and the movement of the door got his attention. He immediately rose to his feet and strode over to her.

"Is Jaicey up to a short visit?" she whispered, doing her best not to stare too fully into Jake's rugged face. He opened the door a bit wider, then gestured for her to turn and go ahead of him out of the room. Marla's heart fell a little as she stepped back into the hall. Jake let the door close behind him and escorted her a bit away from the door to speak.

"She's pretty banged up," he said in a low voice. "One of her friends stopped by a while ago and burst into tears when she saw her, so Jaicey's been pestering for a mirror. One corner of his mouth quirked wryly. "She was almost killed, but she's more worried about her face and hair than she is anything else, so be careful how you act and don't give her a mirror."

Jake must have relaxed enough about his sister's condition to be a little amused by female vanity, and though Marla felt a strong stir of sympathy for Jaicey, she was relieved to hear she was recovered enough to even think of angling for a mirror. Marla took that as a good sign, and it was clear Jake did too.

"Is it all right to see her now?"

"Now's as good a time as any. I can't say how long

she'll be awake, if she still is." He paused and nodded at the quilted bear. "That for her?"

Marla glanced down self-consciously. "I hope she won't think it's too juvenile. I sent flowers, but teddy bears are for…" She hesitated, a little embarrassed. "Teddy bears are for comfort."

Heat surged into her cheeks. The big macho Texan who towered over her would probably find that amusing.

Instead he briefly touched one of the bear's ears. "I reckon this one will," he said, and she felt her heart quake a little at the gruff reassurance. Jake Craddock had a gentle side that affected her far too much. "We'd better go in while she's awake."

Marla preceded him to the door and hesitated when he reached past her to open it. She did her best to conceal her reaction to Jake's nearness. She was here to see her sister, and she had no business letting herself be distracted by anyone, especially Jake.

CHAPTER FIVE

BECAUSE her need to see her sister overcame everything else, Marla quickly moved away from Jake.

The head of Jaicey's bed was elevated, but her right arm and leg were in casts and propped up on pillows. Her eyes were closed, and Marla was relieved to have a few moments to adjust to the stark changes in her face.

And they were stark. If not for Jake's presence to validate Jaicey's identity, Marla might not have guessed this frail woman was her sister.

Dark circles ringed her eyes, and her face was still a little swollen in places and discolored by bruises. Her upper lip was puffy with a red line bisecting it diagonally. The red seams on her forehead and one cheekbone indicated other cuts. Thankfully the marks were smooth and would eventually fade to barely discernable scars, no doubt due to the work of a skilled plastic surgeon. The red line on the shaved part of her scalp was thicker but would also fade, and be concealed when Jaicey's hair grew back in.

Marla's heart twisted with sympathy and she felt the sting of tears. It was one thing to know that for her, what Jaicey looked like didn't matter; it was another to be confronted with lingering evidence of harsh injuries and the raw pain they must have inflicted, and probably still did.

As if he sensed her dismay, Jake placed his hand on her shoulder and gave it a firm squeeze. She couldn't tell whether he'd done it to warn that Jaicey could open her eyes any moment, or whether it was meant to console. She'd been so focused on noting the changes in Jaicey and trying to cope with her upset about them that she'd temporarily forgotten him.

Not wanting to be distracted by him now, Marla stepped closer to the head of the bed. She set her handbag and the bear on the bed table and did her best to compose herself. Jaicey looked asleep, so Marla took care not to startle her. She whispered softly.

"Jaicey? Are you awake?"

At first, Jaicey started to turn her head before pain stopped her and made her catch her breath. After a moment, her eyelids cracked open and slowly lifted. It seemed to take great effort for her to focus on Marla's face and when she did, Marla smiled.

"Hi," she whispered. "How are you feeling?"

Jaicey's eyes were bloodshot, but it was the utter lack of response in them that gave Marla a jolt, as if her presence at the bedside was no more significant than if she'd been a nurse or technician.

"Awful."

At least that answer was in line with Jaicey's usual candor. Marla smiled a little more, trying to take encouragement from that.

"I'll bet. But I'm told you're doing a lot better."

Now Jaicey frowned, at least as much of a frown as her battered face could manage.

"I guess."

Marla couldn't mistake Jaicey's odd remoteness, as if she was suddenly leery of her visitor. Marla felt a nettle of hurt but reminded herself that Jaicey had been through a lot, so that was probably why she seemed so different and aloof. She had to be on pain medication, which could also play a large part in this.

It might be better if she kept this visit even shorter than she'd planned, but the disappointment she felt about leaving so soon was nothing compared to Jaicey's need for rest.

"I brought you something," she said with gentle cheer, then reached for the bear and held it so Jaicey could see. "A get well bear to keep you company."

Jaicey's gaze wavered only a little toward the bear, as if she felt obligated to look before her gaze shifted back to Marla. Though she looked weary, there was a strange intensity in the way she studied Marla's face.

It was a look Marla hadn't seen before, and it made her deeply uneasy. As much as she'd suffered the wait to see her sister, the strange way Jaicey looked at her made her panicky.

And then she sensed what was coming. It was a testament to how well and how deeply she and Jaicey had connected, but for the first time the ability to read her sister caused a feeling of fear instead of a feeling of closeness.

"I'd better not keep you awake any longer," Marla said, suddenly desperate to escape but just as desperate to hide her dismay over her sister's wary scrutiny and somehow prevent the disaster she sensed hovering. "You'll probably want a nap before they bring your supper." She set the bear on the bed table, but her attention snapped back when Jaicey spoke.

"Who…are you?"

Though Marla had sensed it coming, the question hit her hard. "What was that?"

The question was a polite sham. She'd heard Jaicey clearly but hoped against hope that she was wrong.

Jaicey was still studying her with that odd intensity, as if she was trying to place her. Surely she would in a moment. Surely…

"What's your name?"

The words came out weakly and slow, but there was no mistaking them. Marla struggled to answer as her brain tried to deny what this meant. The moments stretched. Jake stepped to her side and leaned past her to get Jaicey's attention. His low voice was calm.

"This is Marla Norris, darlin'. She just moved here from Chicago. She's a friend."

Jaicey appeared to think that over, and then she seemed to relax.

"Oh…your friend."

She looked at Marla, apparently satisfied with that though she still looked wary. Jake's chuckle was slightly forced, as if he meant to keep things light, but Marla sensed his concern. Since no one had mentioned amnesia, Jaicey's inability to remember her might be as much of a surprise for him as it was for her.

"She's more your friend than mine," he said gently. "You've brought her to the ranch a few times, remember?"

Because she was obviously more at ease with Jake than with Marla, Jaicey kept looking at him. Her gaze never went to Marla again.

"No."

Jake reached over the bed rail to give his sister's hand a reassuring pat. "That's all right, sis. No reason to worry about it now. Why don't you rest a while? I'll be close if you need something."

Jaicey gave a long, slow blink and Marla could tell she'd reached the limit of her strength. In the next moment, her eyelids dropped closed and she drifted off.

Marla stood at the bedside, unable to move. It had never entered her mind to think that Jaicey wouldn't know her. The bond between them had grown so strong and so deep that it was hard to believe anything short of death could break it.

Her heart pounded heavily as loss crept through her.

Being forgotten was a unique pain, and in this case, one with startling consequences. She'd come to believe she and Jaicey would always have each other. Since they were both young, there'd been no reason to believe they wouldn't have a long life of closeness. The wreck had temporarily shaken that belief but Jaicey had survived. They'd been on their way to going on together from here. Until this.

Though she hadn't exerted herself, Marla felt out of breath. Her heart was pounding harder and a roaring sound had started in her ears. Everything was badly blurred, and she felt choked.

Jake watched Marla's profile. She was pale beneath the light tan she'd acquired since the last time he'd seen her. He couldn't miss the faint tremor that shook her or the tiny twitch that pulled at the corner of her mouth. He'd seen Jaicey do that when she was trying not to cry, but that was a female thing.

He reached for the call button to summon a nurse, then took hold of Marla's arm to lead her away from the bed. At first, she was stiff and he felt her momentary resistance before she submitted to his silent prompt.

As they turned, he caught sight of her handbag and snagged it as he walked her away from the bed. A nurse bustled in and Jake paused to speak to her. Marla pulled out of his grip and stood a little out of the way.

"Jaicey didn't remember her friend here," he said. "That hasn't happened with anyone else."

The nurse nodded her understanding, then went over to briskly check her patient and efficiently take her vital signs. Jaicey stirred but didn't awaken as the nurse slipped on the blood pressure cuff and began to inflate it as she talked quietly to Jake.

"Some people not only don't remember their accident or what led up to it, but they might lose a chunk of time that we don't find out about at first. I'll give the doctor a call and see what he thinks."

She stopped and adjusted the earpieces of the stethoscope, pumped the cuff tighter, then waited silently as she took the reading. When she pulled the stethoscope from her ears, she went on.

"The doctor's still in the hospital, so he might even stop by. We'll see."

Jake felt relief at the nurse's matter-of-fact tone. A small movement in his side vision drew his gaze to where Marla stood, gripping the back of the chair he'd sat in that afternoon. She still looked pale and shaken up over Jaicey's inability to recognize her, and her hazel gaze was fixed on Jaicey's face.

Her reaction to all this was strong, maybe too strong. It seemed strange to him, but he didn't really know her. Yes, it had probably thrown her for a loop when Jaicey hadn't known her, but she looked devastated, which didn't exactly fit his impression of her friendship with his sister.

On the other hand, women friends were a lot different than men friends, and they got into each other's business more than men did. They were also a lot more emotional about each other. No doubt Marla was just like most women, and her reaction only seemed too much to him because she and Jaicey hadn't known each other long.

It could even be that Jaicey was the only close friend Marla had made here so far, which brought him back briefly to the idea that Marla Norris was too hard to figure. And right now he had too many things on his mind to bother with anything but Jaicey.

Marla watched the nurse check Jaicey over. The woman didn't show even a flicker of alarm, but Marla couldn't take much comfort from that. Nurses were too good at keeping calm. She gripped the chair back and felt so shaky she wished she had the nerve to sit down, but she already felt like an intruder with Jake standing by. She couldn't bring herself to leave yet, not until she knew something more. Tears burned as she stared at Jaicey, willing her to be all right. She looked so fragile.

Please, God, I'd rather she never remembered me at all than to have this mean she's gotten worse. Please don't let her die...

Aware that Jake might soon express some kind of disapproval of her hanging around in the room, she didn't look his way. No doubt he was just as preoccupied with

Jaicey's condition and what the nurse was saying as she was. He had to be at least as upset as she was over this, so neither of them were at their best or most tactful. She felt for him though. She'd known and loved her sister for little more than six months, but he'd known and loved Jaicey all her life. This had to be even harder on him than it was on her.

Marla wished she could say so, but she also wished there was some way to let him know she had just as much right to sit with Jaicey as he did, wished they could console and encourage each other like families did in times of trouble. But those were selfish wishes, motivated by her own craving for comfort. And nothing good ever came from wishing anyway, not with important things. Hadn't she learned not to depend on anyone but herself?

As Marla stood there looking on, trying not to hope for anything but Jaicey's full recovery, she realized she couldn't so much as hint that she was Jaicey's twin. Jaicey hadn't been ready to tell the Craddocks about her before the wreck, and now that she couldn't remember, there was no rush for anyone else to know.

The accident had been hard on the Craddocks, particularly on Judd, and Marla felt certain Jaicey want to continue their secret until things more or less returned to normal. She'd already decided that if Jaicey didn't make it, there was really nothing to be gained by telling the Craddocks. Though she'd never considered the possibility that Jaicey would forget her, keeping silent seemed the only sensible thing to do.

The burning in her eyes got worse, and Marla did her best to keep the tears back. This wasn't the time for tears, not with Jake around to see them. She was the friend he didn't quite approve of, so he might consider tears too over the top.

The nurse went out and Marla moved away from the chair, intending to step into the hall and find some privacy. She realized then that she didn't have her handbag, but Jake turned to her and held it out.

"You look like you should sit down," he said as she took the bag and settled the strap on her shoulder.

"I'm fine."

She tried a smile that felt so transparently fake that she let it shrink away. She wasn't quite brave enough to look him in the eye for fear she'd give herself away.

"Would you mind if I waited down the hall until the nurse has some word? I hate to leave before I know for sure Jaicey's okay."

"Suit yourself. It shouldn't be long."

Marla murmured a soft, "Thanks," then left the room to go to the waiting room, doing her best to keep herself together. She was grateful to have the room to herself as she tried to get past her shock.

Jake's visit to the waiting room later was brief. According to the doctor, Jaicey's condition hadn't changed so much as it had become more clear. Pending more extensive tests, it was the doctor's opinion that Jaicey had lost not only her memory of the wreck and the hours leading up to it, but she'd also lost the past few months, perhaps as much as a year.

He'd awakened Jaicey and asked about community events in the past few months, but Jaicey's recollections fit last summer more closely than this summer. Though the doctor stressed that his initial impression could be mistaken pending more tests, it seemed to explain why Jake and Judd and a handful of long-term friends had been remembered, but Marla had not.

It was a relief to know the doctor didn't believe Jaicey's condition had gotten worse. Though he'd said this lapse might be only temporary, he'd also said the partial memory loss could be permanent.

Some reaction that had made it past her carefully neutral expression must have alerted Jake, because he'd tried to soften that last bit of information.

His gruff, "You and Jaicey were fast friends before, so it could happen again," was anything but reassuring to a heart that had learned to be far less optimistic. Marla had smiled as if she agreed with his pronouncement and thanked him for putting her mind at ease about Jaicey's condition.

By the time she got home, Marla wasn't hungry enough to bother with food. She didn't feel like working on the quilt, either, so she decided to go to the store to rent a DVD. None of the titles appealed to her, so she drove home and watched part of a movie on cable before she gave up and went to bed.

That next week, she worked harder than ever at the law office to keep her mind occupied. She now called Miss Jenny at Craddock Ranch for updates on Jaicey, but she hadn't gone to visit at the hospital.

There wasn't much she could say to prompt Jaicey to remember, and since Jake or Judd were always nearby to overhear, she couldn't risk it. More important, Jaicey needed every scrap of her energy and focus to recover, and Marla refused to add to her difficulties.

The good part was that Jaicey wouldn't still be worrying about how the Craddocks would take their secret. The bad part was that she'd have no interest in visits from someone she couldn't remember. It was hard to face the idea that Jaicey might not remember on her own, but once she got well enough to go home, she might find something there to remind her.

Marla thought about the photo album. Had it survived the wreck? Jaicey had given her their documentation to keep at the apartment, so Marla had no idea what else Jaicey might have besides the album.

Remembering the album made it easier for Marla to be patient and keep away from the hospital, but that lasted only a few days. After that, she missed her sister even more and longed to see for herself how she was doing.

Was it possible to drop by the hospital for a friendly visit? Take a bouquet along as an excuse to say hello?

Jaicey was the outgoing type who never met a stranger, but the memory of her remoteness and her obvious wariness that day at the hospital made Marla leery of even a brief visit. The last thing she wanted was to make Jaicey uncomfortable or put her off.

It was best to stay away. As much as it hurt, at least it was a hurt Jaicey didn't have to bear. Marla consoled herself with the idea that this wasn't forever. Someday soon Jaicey would be well enough to be reminded she had a sister. Until then, Marla would have to do her best to wait for that time.

CHAPTER SIX

NONE of them had heard much from Marla, except when she called Miss Jenny for news every couple of days. His father had remarked on that more than once, which reminded Jake that she hadn't been part of the almost constant parade of friends to Jaicey's hospital room. As strong as he'd thought her reaction to Jaicey's amnesia had been, her absence since then was a surprise.

He hadn't phoned Marla himself, and after his last visit to her apartment, he'd decided it wasn't a good idea to see her alone. He still had no reasonable explanation for the sudden desire that had come over him that night. One moment they were standing just inside her door, the next he'd pulled her close.

He shouldn't have done that, but it had happened so spontaneously that it must have been instinct. He'd managed to explain it away later, figuring he'd been tired and worried and tense enough to want some kind of soothing. His body had simply reacted to the late hour, the soft light, and the desirable young woman he'd been holding hands with.

If she hadn't backed away and rushed him out the door, there was no telling what more might have happened. Since he prided himself on his good sense and his sexual self-control, he'd been a little shocked to lose track of both for those few moments. By the next morning, he'd decided to keep a comfortable distance from the mysterious Miss Norris.

Now that he'd had more than a month of success, he found himself thinking about her. It was midmorning on a Saturday, and he'd planned to stop at the hospital to say hello to his sister before he made a few other stops. Since Miss Connie liked to visit Jaicey until about one o'clock, Jake was in no rush to interrupt and considered making a few of those stops now. Besides, most of Jaicey's friends came by on the weekends, so he hadn't planned to visit long today anyway.

Maybe that was why he was thinking about Marla. He told himself that the impulse to drop by her place was simple curiosity, but when he sounded the buzzer at her building, she didn't answer. She was probably out on errands like most folks on Saturdays, so he left.

Since Marla's apartment was near the east side of Coulter City, he took a side trip just past the city limits. A new supercab pickup had caught his eye the other day at the dealership he preferred, and he meant to drive by to see if it was still on the lot.

Instead a spot of color along the gravel road that intersected the highway got his attention. The road coming up unofficially served as a dividing line between town and country, but it was unusual for anyone to be walking there unless they had car trouble.

The spot of dark pink that looked like a hat stood out against the backdrop of rangeland and blue sky beyond. As he drove closer to the turnoff, he saw more of the woman who wore the hat. At first, it looked like she was pacing back and forth at the side of the road, but then she suddenly grabbed off the hat and rushed into the shallow ditch.

Concerned, Jake braked to turn off the pavement onto the gravel. He'd taken the turn too fast and the pickup fishtailed on the loose rock before the tire treads bit in. As he sped closer to the woman, recognition dawned.

The life or death drama in the grassy ditch felt as if it had been going on for hours instead of a few minutes. Two small kittens, who didn't look much bigger than hamsters, were struggling through the tall, sun-seared grass.

She'd seen them several feet ahead of her along the road, but when she'd walked closer they'd seen her and run for cover. Marla had crossed to their side of the road, anxious to find them. They were too tiny to be out here alone. They'd be prey to any animal, large or small, and she hadn't had the heart to walk on.

When she reached the place where she'd last seen them, Marla heard a rustling in the grass and a plaintive meow. She tried to coax the babies out of the grass, but they ventured only close enough for her to see them. The poor little things had either gotten lost from their mother or been dumped out along the road, and they were too afraid to come within reach.

It was then that another movement in the grass drew her attention, and she briefly glimpsed the diamond pattern of a large snake. To her horror, it was moving toward the kittens. She urgently repeated the soft kitty-kitty call she'd being trying, but the kittens hung back, afraid.

She tried to think of a quick way to lure them out, but another glimpse of the snake—closer now—made her grab off her hat and hurry into the ditch to save them. The dry grass brushed high against her ankles and knees, the contact making her even more aware that she was vulnerable to snakebite, but she couldn't bring herself to abandon the kittens. At least they had trouble running from her in the tall grass, so she was able to work her way closer.

She was terrified the snake—a *rattlesnake!*—would get close enough to strike at her bare ankles, so she stomped her feet a little hoping to sound more menacing. The frantic wave of her hat was meant to shoo the snake away, but unfortunately, the only creatures in the ditch it frightened were the kittens.

The rattler did stop moving forward, though, and

Marla kept an eye on it while she walked gingerly after the kittens. Her relief that the snake had stopped his pursuit was short-lived when she saw it begin to coil defensively. The dry rattling sound that came next was so loud to her terror-sharp nerves that it seemed to echo after the first few seconds.

She also heard the sound of an engine and the splatter of gravel as a vehicle sped down the road toward her. Because the ditch was only three feet deep, she was certain she'd been seen. The vehicle slowed and came to a sliding stop behind her, but she kept moving slowly through the ditch, determined to catch the kittens and escape before the snake showed any more aggression. At least someone else was nearby, and could possibly help.

The truck engine switched off, the door opened. Over the ticking of the heated engine, Marla heard an odd sound before a door clicked closed, as if the driver wanted to avoid slamming it. The crunch of heavy boots on gravel was brisk as the man—it could only be a man—strode to the edge of the road somewhere behind her. The low growl of a male voice startled her already frazzled nerves.

"Stop there and don't move."

Marla recognized Jake's voice and froze.

"You've got two rattlers—no, dammit, don't look!"

Marla's heart rate shot up yet again and she almost fainted. *Two* rattlesnakes? *Where?* Her mouth was so dry with terror that she almost couldn't speak.

"K-kittens…I've got kittens," she called out softly.

A swear word was his initial reply to that. "Where?"

"Just in front of me, maybe four feet?"

Another swear word, then, "I'll get 'em in a minute. Don't move."

The loud report of a handgun made her jump. She squealed and did a little hop when a second report sent a small shower of dirt and gravel against her ankles. She'd started to bolt, but a hard, strong arm hooked around her waist.

"Of all the damned fool things to get into," he roared, then abruptly let her go.

Marla half turned, stumbling in fresh terror before Jake caught her wrist to steady her. She looked up fearfully into a harsh face that was dark with temper. Black eyes glittered down at her from beneath his hat brim.

"Are they dead?" She glanced frantically around her feet, but a tug on her wrist made her gaze leap back up to his.

"You little fool, traipsing in here with sneakers and bare legs. If one of those snakes had bit you—"

"Kittens," she got out. "There are kittens. I c-couldn't let them be—"

She'd started to look down and away toward the kittens, but instead caught sight of the handgun Jake was holding. It looked like a cannon, and her words had choked off. Her ears were still ringing from the gunshots, but her eyes felt as big as saucers as she stared stupidly at the weapon.

Jake seemed to realize the sight of the gun had startled her into silence. He clicked on the safety and hooked it in his belt.

"Kittens? Kittens are a dime a dozen, and so are rattlers," he ranted on. "You're all this way out here, God knows why, and if one of those snakes had nailed you, you'd be dead before anyone could notice and get you to a hospital."

Marla's nerves were still jangling. "I couldn't let the snake—"

"Ra*ttlers*," he interrupted curtly. "More than one. Look."

Marla couldn't help obeying the sharp order, and looked in the direction he'd indicated. The nearness of the dead snake made her flinch away and lunge for the safety of Jake's big body. She grabbed his shirt just above his waist as she looked back at the snake that lay in two harmless pieces. Her brain didn't quite grasp that it wouldn't somehow spring to life and strike. Jake's voice was terse.

"Where are they?"

She looked up at him, dazed. Her head was swimming, but she glanced toward where she'd last seen the kittens.

"Over there," she said, finding the courage to let go of his shirt and point.

Jake immediately started in that direction, his big boots tromping down the grass. Irrationally afraid he'd be too rough with the kittens or be careless enough in his anger to step on them, Marla lurched after him and caught his arm.

"Please—don't hurt them! They're so tiny and afraid."

Jake stopped and his dark gaze flashed down sharply into hers. Outrage had turned his angry expression stony, and that frightened her even more.

"Please, don't take it out on them," she urged, getting a tighter grip on his arm so she could stop him if she had to.

Suddenly she was a child again, in a bad place where anger ruled and the small and the weak needed protection. A little boy's face flashed in her mind. The awful memory was one of many she'd worked hard to forget, but the tight anger on Jake's face had brought it back with a vengeance.

Anger, particularly male anger, was dangerous to children and small creatures. Marla had to fight to remember she wasn't in that bad place anymore.

The look that crossed Jake's face was one of surprise before his harsh features eased a bit. His dark gaze was still glittering, but with less anger, and she saw the sharp curiosity in the dark lights. Marla stared up at him, still reeling from the memory and his abrupt change as she mentally reviewed her words and realized how hard she gripped his arm. Her fingernails were literally dug in and she made her fingers relax and belatedly pulled her hands away.

"So-orry," she stammered out, horrified at how quickly

she'd overreacted, but even more horrified when she saw that she'd left bright curved marks on his forearm. The fact that she hadn't broken the skin was small comfort.

Jake turned from her without a word and searched the ditch.

Marla rubbed her palms over her flushed face as if she could scrub away both the old trauma and the new. She hadn't thought about Tommy for years, and she didn't need to think about that awful time.

All she had to remember was that she'd saved him, and he'd finally gone to a good family. Her brain had probably made a connection between Tommy and the kittens, then started to make other connections.

Marla lowered her hands in time to see Jake bend down. He plucked the kittens out of the grass, and easily fit the squirming, meowing bits of fur into one hand. He glanced around, brushing his broad palm over the top of the grass as he continued to look through it.

Her nerves had time to calm a little more as she'd watched. Jake held the kittens easily, gently. She was so relieved that she felt light-headed.

"Where are the others?" His voice was almost soft now and Marla felt twisting shame for thinking even for a moment that he was a monster.

"I only saw two," she said. She hadn't seen others, but since litters were usually bigger than two, there might be more. She hadn't given it a thought.

Jake turned, still looking through the grass as he did,

then handed the terrified kittens to her without looking
at her face. She took the kittens, who were a lot more
difficult for her to hold onto because she was afraid
she'd hurt them. Their little bodies felt like small hanks
of fur stretched over toothpicks. They must be starving.

"Take 'em to the truck and I'll have a look around.
Turn the key in the ignition and get the air conditioner
going so you don't bake, but don't let them get chilled."

Marla started up the bank of the shallow ditch to the
road, clutching the kittens against her and despite her
great relief, she was shaking almost as hard from reaction as they were. She went to the passenger side of the
pickup, carefully climbed in, then reached over to
switch on the engine.

Jake had been right about the chill, so to keep the kittens warm and to give them a better sense of security,
she pulled the tail of her T-shirt out of her cutoff jeans
and made a hammock out of the hem to wrap them up.
Being able to do that for them helped her feel better.

The babies were the tiniest she'd ever seen. Their fur
was a dull gray, thicker against their bodies, but thin and
wispy at the ends. They'd picked up some sharp little
burrs in the grass, but Marla decided she'd need scis-
sors to cut them out.

The kittens were plain and looked more like mice,
with trembling ears that looked too large for their little
heads. Their faces were different, and one was slightly
bigger than the other. And now they were exhausted,

staring up at her silently, as if they were too tired to fight and were resigned to their fate.

Marla's heart broke over that, and the cool air of the cab made her aware that tears of pity hovered on her lashes. At the same moment the driver's side door opened and she jumped, glancing toward Jake as he tossed her forgotten hat on the seat between them. Before he could see, she jerked up a hand to brush away the tears he'd startled loose.

Her soft, "Thank you," was hoarse. She tried not to make it obvious that she was watching as Jake picked up a holster from the floor on his side and snapped the gun into it. Guns were a necessity at the ranch, and Marla was glad he'd had one in the truck and knew how to use it. Though guns terrified her, she was practical enough to know she'd have been in trouble today without one.

"I—I didn't see the other snake," she said, still bewildered about that, but also overcome with the old need to explain herself in a way that would mollify him.

And truly, the snake had been so close that she didn't understand how she'd missed it. "When the other one started rattling, I thought it was just fear that made me hear it all ov—"

"From now on, where you see one rattler, figure there's at least one more," he cut in sternly as he shoved the holstered gun under his seat. "Where's your car?"

Dismayed that Jake was still angry, Marla's gaze

shot to his and she saw she was mistaken. Jake looked relaxed, with only a trace of the angry man he'd been in the ditch, though she sensed his anger could easily come thundering back. But did she truly sense that, or was she still caught up in old memories?

"I was out for a walk. It was a nice day and not too hot yet."

Jake's dark brows lowered in instant disapproval. "You've got miles of pavement in town if you want to walk. Being dressed like that, you're asking for trouble, from critters *and* two-legged varmints up to no good."

He'd paused to emphasize that last part, as if she was completely naïve and he meant to scare her.

"If this was Chicago," he went on a little scornfully, "I'll bet you'd be more careful where you walked."

Marla could only stare at him, wary again because he was angry with her. As if he realized it, he faced forward and expelled a short, annoyed breath.

"The kittens can go to the ranch. I'll have the vet take a look at 'em first, and if he doesn't want to put them up for adoption at the clinic, we might have a momma cat at one of the barns who'll take 'em."

Marla looked quickly down at the babies, who were now fast asleep. One had weeping eyes that had dampened and matted the fur on its face and they both had dirty little ears, which meant they weren't the best candidates for care from a mother they hadn't been born to.

Marla knew all about how choosy some foster moms could be.

The thought of the kittens being turned loose in a barn with a mother cat who might or might not accept them was one she immediately rejected, but she was hesitant to say so just now, or explain why. If the vet would see that they were adopted, that would be better.

But as she carefully stroked a fingertip over one tiny head then the other, she felt her heart break a little more, unable to keep from remembering the way they'd looked up at her a few moments ago. They were tiny, helpless creatures, too small and too weak to fight or to even object to anything she might do to them or allow to be done.

And she'd seen the hopelessness in their eyes. Maybe they would have looked at the rattlesnake that same way when it had got to them and they knew they couldn't escape. They were just as much at her mercy now, and the need to protect them was suddenly strong. Just like it had been with little Tommy when they'd been alone and without protection.

"If they're adopted, would they be adopted together?" she ventured.

"Usually not, but the vet would see they'd get good homes with folks who love cats."

The idea of splitting up the babies troubled her. They would be less lonely if they were kept together, and they could protect each other. *She* could protect them. "I love cats."

She'd never had one, but the few she'd been around had been so fascinating and fun that she'd envied the kids who had cats but took them for granted. She felt a stir of excitement as she seriously considered keeping them. If she did, she'd never wonder if they were being taken care of.

"You ever have a cat?"

Marla heard the skepticism in his low voice, and she was a little taken aback that he'd ask if she'd ever had a cat. Could he tell?

"No," she said, then looked over at him. "But I want these."

"What about your building? Are cats allowed?"

Jake sounded like a social worker grilling an overeager child who hadn't thought ahead. She looked down at the kittens, too possessive about them now to care.

"There's an extra deposit. If they don't like that I have more than one, I can move."

She'd been saving money for years to make a down payment on a house of her own. And she'd already checked real estate prices here and was certain she could find a small place she could afford. She'd not done that from the beginning because she was from out of state and she'd wanted to see how she liked Coulter City and how things worked out with the Craddocks.

And yet the idea of buying a house just so she could have pets was a shock. She wasn't impulsive, but the kittens had affected her usually cautious temperament, tapping into something inside that she couldn't ignore.

She sensed it when Jake looked over at her and she glanced his way. No doubt he thought she was crazy— he couldn't possibly guess that what she'd done and planned to do made perfect sense—but his expression showed little more than irritable resignation.

"Then you'd better let the vet look 'em over. If you take them home like that, you're gonna have a flea infestation. One's got an eye infection, and they've probably got ear mites and worms."

Jake faced forward again, checked the mirrors and put the truck into gear. He made a three-point turn on the gravel and drove back to the highway. Marla spoke up, relieved he'd accepted her decision so quickly, but forced to think about practical things.

"Do you mean we should go to the vet now? I'll need to go home to get my checkbook, and I can't take up any more of your time with this." Particularly since it was obvious he felt put upon.

"It's my time," he groused, "and the clinic closes by noon. If you don't get there now, you might have to wait till Monday. Like I said, you don't want a flea infestation at your place. And don't worry about your checkbook. This first trip to the vet's on me."

Marla shook her head, adamant. "Thank you, but no. I'll ask if he can bill me or I'll write you a check to cover the cost when I get home."

"Suit yourself."

His tone said the conversation was over. Marla watched

his profile for a few moments more. Though his expression was indifferent, she sensed that his irritation and disapproval hadn't eased much. She'd always been hypersensitive to those things and she hated that her first thought was to do or say something that would somehow earn his approval. She had no idea what that would take anyway, and it was sure to be a waste of time to try to figure it out.

CHAPTER SEVEN

THE veterinarian turned out to be a cat expert. And it wasn't the older male vet who examined the kittens, but the new lady vet who'd joined the clinic as a fourth partner earlier in the year.

It pleased Marla when Jake went into one of the examination rooms with her and the kittens, but when she got a look at the new vet, she guessed meeting her was the real reason Jake had offered to go in with them.

Dr. Brownlee was a very attractive brunette who came from a family of veterinarians. Jake apparently had heard of her father, and the two spoke briefly before the doctor got down to business. The vet's routine helped banish any wisp of dark feelings that lingered, and took Marla's mind completely off the past.

The male kitten weighed fourteen ounces, and the female only ten ounces. The vet whisked them away to remove the burrs and treat them with a product that killed fleas and ear mites. They were far too young for vacci-

GET FREE BOOKS and a FREE GIFT WHEN YOU PLAY THE...

Just scratch off the silver box with a coin. Then check below to see the gifts you get!

SLOT MACHINE GAME!

YES! I have scratched off the silver box. Please send me the 2 free Harlequin Romance® books and gift for which I qualify. I understand I am under no obligation to purchase any books, as explained on the back of this card.

386 HDL D74E   186 HDL EEZ5

FIRST NAME

LAST NAME

ADDRESS

APT.#

CITY

STATE/PROV.

ZIP/POSTAL CODE

7	7	7	**Worth TWO FREE BOOKS plus a BONUS Mystery Gift!**
🍒	🍒	🍒	**Worth TWO FREE BOOKS!**
♣	♣	♣	**Worth ONE FREE BOOK!**
🔔	🔔	🍒	**TRY AGAIN!**

www.eHarlequin.com

(H-R-02/06)

DETACH AND MAIL CARD TODAY!

The Harlequin Reader Service® — Here's how it works:

Accepting your 2 free books and gift places you under no obligation to buy anything. You may keep the books and gift and return the shipping statement marked "cancel." If you do not cancel, about a month later we'll send you 6 additional books and bill you just $3.57 each in the U.S., or $4.05 each in Canada, plus 25¢ shipping & handling per book and applicable taxes if any.* That's the complete price and — compared to cover prices of $4.25 each in the U.S. and $4.99 each in Canada — it's quite a bargain! You may cancel at any time, but if you choose to continue, every month we'll send you 6 more books, which you may either purchase at the discount price or return to us and cancel your subscription.

*Terms and prices subject to change without notice. Sales tax applicable in N.Y. Canadian residents will be charged applicable provincial taxes and GST. Credit or debit balances in a customer's account(s) may be offset by any other outstanding balance owed by or to the customer.

If offer card is missing write to: Harlequin Reader Service, 3010 Walden Ave., P.O. Box 1867, Buffalo NY 14240-1867

BUSINESS REPLY MAIL
FIRST-CLASS MAIL   PERMIT NO. 717-003   BUFFALO, NY

POSTAGE WILL BE PAID BY ADDRESSEE

HARLEQUIN READER SERVICE
3010 WALDEN AVE
PO BOX 1867
BUFFALO NY 14240-9952

NO POSTAGE
NECESSARY
IF MAILED
IN THE
UNITED STATES

nations, but they had their first round of deworming. After the vet determined they were barely six weeks old, she said their tiny size was due to severe malnourishment. The doctor gave Marla eye drops for the female kitten, and told her about the kitten milk formula she could buy at the pet store to supplement the dry and canned cat food brand she recommended.

By the time they were finished and Jake had written out a hefty check, the kittens were snuggling their trembling little bodies against Marla. The examination had traumatized them. When she and Jake got back to the pickup, Marla tucked the babies into the crown of her cloth hat and they settled instantly into exhausted sleep.

Jake hadn't said much and neither had she, except for the questions she'd asked the vet. She was beginning to think he was counting the minutes until he could be rid of her, when he unexpectedly turned into a shopping center on the way to the apartment and parked in front of a large pet store. Marla looked over at him, surprised.

"I didn't realize where we were going, but this is over and above what you should be doing for us. It's very, very nice, and very thoughtful," she said to soften her coming refusal, "but we've taken up enough of your day."

The "us" and "we" felt natural to say and Marla felt the tug on her heart. *Us.* Not a concept she'd had a lot of experience with, but one she was assured of with the kittens. Her heart felt lighter when she realized that, but

Jake glanced her way, his dark brows knit together again, spoiling it.

"You seem to have firm ideas about how I spend my time."

Marla stared, not sure if that was a criticism or not. "I appreciate very much what you've done, but you must have had other plans. Plus, Jaicey must be expecting you at the hospital. And I still don't have my checkbook. I can't leave the kittens in the truck when it's so hot."

The hasty list should have been enough to convince him to take her straight home, but she was mystified when it was not.

"This store invites folks to bring their pets in," he told her, "and the kittens might like to see the birds."

With that, Jake opened his door and got out to come around to her side of the pickup. As at the vet's, he helped her out of the tall vehicle. Though she wasn't comfortable doing this, the moment they got into the big pet store, she was distracted by the sheer abundance and variety it offered, including pets for sale. From reptiles to birds, mice and hamsters to rabbits, fish of all kinds, as well as a couple of puppies and three kittens.

She'd started to carry the kittens in the hat since the hat wasn't thick enough to cushion them from the hard wire of the cart, but Jake put one of the little shopping baskets in the cart, took the kittens out of the hat, then folded it to provide enough padding for the babies to continue their nap.

His solution made her smile, but she didn't remark on how reluctantly domestic he looked as he pushed the cart along for her. She guessed it wasn't something he'd had much experience doing, and she liked that he did it. It was as if he was trying to make up for his temper, when he probably thought nothing of it, and making things up to her was the last thing on his mind.

The kittens didn't finish their nap, and scrambled over each other to see above the top of the basket. They were trembling again, and Marla felt bad. She picked them up and cuddled them against her so they could look around, and they gradually grew quiet.

They were very interested in watching the caged birds, perking up a bit before the trauma of the day caught up with them. The tiny female fell asleep watching and the little male snuggled closer to his sister and did the same.

Once they got to the cat aisles, Marla found the formula, the dry and canned food the vet had recommended, and a pair of small food and water dishes. She added two kitten-size litter pans, a scoop, litter and a scratching post. Jake pointed out a couple of tiny nursing bottles in case they were needed, as well as the section of cat toys.

Marla bought a few of the toys, as well as a soft brush for the kitten's rough little coats. She rejected buying a cat bed, instead looking them over so she could make one later. She also elected to wait to buy a cat carrier for trips to the vet. Jake found a book on kittens and cats, then later paid for it separately and gave it to her in the truck.

At last they were on their way and Marla couldn't help feeling a little let down that their time together was coming quickly to an end.

It was just as well. She cuddled the kittens closer and tried to remember if she had a cardboard box that would serve as a temporary place for the babies to sleep until she could make them a proper cat bed.

It was after two o'clock by the time they got to her apartment. Jake let her off at the back door of her building so he could park the pickup. Marla went inside and immediately unlocked and opened the patio door. While she found a medium-size box to corral the kittens in and placed a thick towel inside for them to sleep on, Jake brought in the shopping bags.

Even more aware of how much of his time she'd taken up, Marla quickly wrote out a check to reimburse him for the vet visit and the trip to the pet store. By the time she brought the check to him from the kitchen, Jake was crouched beside the kitten box gently petting them.

Marla suddenly felt nervous. She'd written out the check for the amount he'd spent on the kittens, but it didn't seem nearly enough. He'd be offended if she paid him more money than she owed, so she needed to repay him in another way. Now could be the perfect time to invite him to dinner, or to at least feed him a nice late lunch. She could even buy him lunch if he'd rather eat out. Of course, that would take even more of his time, but she at least had to offer.

On the other hand, it could be that he'd had more than had enough of her and wouldn't want her to so much as fix him a sandwich. At least he wasn't hovering by the door as if he couldn't wait to get away. She took a steadying breath and tried to keep this light.

"Would you like me to fix you a quick lunch? Or if you'd give me a few minutes to shower and change, I could take you out somewhere, my treat. After everything you've done today, you deserve more than to just get your money back."

Jake looked up at her. "How 'bout we make coffee and get the babies set up, have you shower and change while they eat, then *I* take *you* out? After that, you'd probably need to get back so the kittens know you haven't abandoned them."

Marla was so surprised that her mouth started to drop open before she caught herself. This was far more than the grudging agreement she'd expected. And there wasn't so much as a trace of his earlier irritation and impatience. He'd lost those things sometime in the pet store, and now he was completely mellow. His dark eyes held hers and she instantly felt the strong pull of attraction between them. She scrambled to collect herself and resist it, but only the habit of never owing anyone brought her back to earth.

"Only if it's my treat," she said, managing to sound adamant about that. She wished she felt as adamant about resisting her attraction to Jake. "I can't possibly thank you enough for rescuing us and doing all the rest."

One corner of his handsome mouth quirked up, as if he realized she was flustered. "Whatever you say."

The lazy way he said that made her heart flutter, but she handed him the check, which he folded without reading and slipped into his shirt pocket as he straightened to his full height. He'd already upended his Stetson on the coffee table and now reached for the shopping bags.

"Where do you want to set this stuff up?"

"I need to start the coffee, so I suppose in the kitchen," she said, then glanced into the box. The kittens were still sleeping, so she led the way.

Marla divided the cat things between kitchen, living room and bathroom. Once the kittens were fed, they'd need access to a litter pan. After she washed the tiny bottles and new cat dishes, she made up a batch of formula in a small plastic pitcher with a lid and put some of it into the nursing bottles.

The cat dishes looked too deep for the kittens to use just yet, so she got out a couple of plastic lids with rims. Since babies were still sleeping, she meant to leave Jake in the living room with coffee and a plate of home baked cookies. He helped her carry them in, but before she could rush away, he stopped her.

"By the way, I wasn't exactly mild mannered and understanding this morning," he said. "I apologize. You did a brave thing. I just hope you'll be more careful for yourself next time. There are a lot of dangers in the big outdoors."

The somber look in his eyes said he genuinely meant his apology, and she felt emotion roll through her.

"Thank you," she said, then turned quickly away to walk to the hall. His apology made her feel awkward. She hadn't expected it, and it affected her more deeply than it should. The way he'd worded it had made her feel as if he valued her, but that was nothing to get excited about. He would have flattered any city slicker he hoped would take his admonishment seriously.

As she got fresh clothes from her bedroom and took them with her into the bathroom, she suddenly remembered something Jaicey had said at the hospital, when Jake had to explain who she was.

Oh, your *friend...*

Apparently Jaicey had thought Marla was Jake's friend, no doubt one of the many lady friends he had, because the message in the way she'd said "friend" had meant "girlfriend." The Craddocks were so close that the friend of one would be known by the others, and Jaicey had told her she always made it a point to meet and get to know Jake's girlfriends.

Marla hadn't given Jaicey's mistake a thought until now, but then she hadn't seen Jake since that day. Now they'd crossed paths again, and though they'd gotten off to a bumpy start this morning over the kittens, Jake had completely changed toward her.

She was so struck by the difference in him that she couldn't help wondering, *what if?*

Marla's craving to see her sister was overwhelming in those next seconds. The longing to somehow become part of Jaicey's life again was painfully sharp. Naturally she went back to the impossible notion of "What if?"

What if she became Jake's girlfriend? The question, serious now, made her heart pump with both excitement and anxiety. Her thoughts moved to the next question as she shampooed her hair.

What exactly would being a friend—a girlfriend—of Jake's be like? What would someone like her have to do to even have a chance? And if she somehow got a chance, how far should she be prepared to go? A man like Jake would have expectations, physical ones. Could she put off fulfilling them and still hold his interest?

It couldn't go too far between them because that would be dangerous. Jake was too overwhelming, too male for her to handle easily. Besides, she wasn't rich or glamorous enough for a man like him. They were as opposite as night and day.

And there were no guarantees, no way to ensure that the attraction she felt for Jake wouldn't quickly escalate to more complicated feelings on her part, no matter how hard she tried to control them. After all, everything would have to look genuine.

Marla felt a new shock as she realized how far she was taking this wild idea.

Jake was a worldly man who could have any woman he wanted. He was the kind who chose for himself, the kind who made the first move if he was interested.

And who was she kidding? She probably had something less than a snowball's chance of success, even if Jake allowed her to make the first move.

Frustrated with herself, Marla finished her shower. So much for wild ideas.

It seemed to take a long time to dry her hair, but her light makeup went on in a flash. After she dithered over whether or not to wear a bit of perfume, she used a dab here and there then put on the perky yellow summer dress that showed off her tan, before she stepped into casual sandals.

A fast straightening of the bathroom and she was on her way out to see if the kittens were awake. Jake had them on his lap, gently teasing them with the flexible plastic rod that trailed a cord with feathers on the end. The kittens' play was tentative, and they seemed more interested in staring up into the giant's face than in playing with the toy. Marla noticed right away the empty lids on the coffee table, and that the babies' tummies looked plumper.

"Did they get enough to eat?" she asked.

"Enough for now. They don't look like they're used to much, so it's probably best to feed them a little less than they want, but feed them more often, at least for the first few days."

That made sense to Marla. And Jake seemed to be an expert with animals, so he must know something about cats. After all, she'd seen some around the ranch, though mostly at the barns. The kittens looked contented now, happy to let him trail the feather next to them while they made a shy effort or two to catch it. Marla sat down in the armchair to watch.

It was hard to believe this was the man who'd said that kittens were a dime a dozen. Especially when one of the kittens climbed up his shirtfront to sniff at his chin and he laid a hand over it for gentle support. The kitten immediately snuggled higher to get between his shirt collar and his neck. Once it settled, Jake's big thumb lightly rubbed its head. It touched her to see how tender he was, especially when he picked up the other kitten and nestled it beside the one resting against his neck.

"Kittens usually play a lot, don't they?" she asked. "I expected them to be more active."

"They've been hungry too long, and they're pretty small, more apt to sleep. Give 'em a few days of food and care, and they'll act more normal," he said before he added, "You might want to leave them with a little formula and some of that dry food while we're gone. That way, if they wake up and we're not back yet, they won't go hungry or thirsty. They didn't take to the bottles."

Marla again thought about his "dime a dozen" remark. And it wasn't as if these babies were special or very pretty, not with their ratty gray fur and their lack of a pedigree. In her experience, men didn't care for cats, and she'd believed Jake didn't, either. It was his tenderness with them that changed her mind, and she was fascinated by the idea that a tough, macho man could be so gentle and affectionate with such tiny creatures.

It seemed genuine, and Marla felt herself fall a little in love with him. The moment she realized it, she abruptly got to her feet. The instinct to resist these almost diabolical feelings was as automatic as it was sharp.

"I'll just get them a little more formula and food, then close them in the bathroom with their things."

She picked up the lids and took them for a refill before she carried them down the hall to the bathroom. Jake trailed after her with the kittens and brought along the box with the towel.

She'd already placed one of the litter pans in the bathroom, so she set the food lids next to the bathtub while Jake set the box on its side in the laundry area. Putting the box on the floor that way insured that the kittens could go in and out as they liked. He handed her the babies, then reached to close the air-conditioning vent halfway so the room wouldn't get too cool.

"Do they know how to use their litter pan?" she asked.

"It's instinct," he said as she set the kittens down and they immediately began to investigate the room. "They'll figure it out."

Once she and Jake washed up, Marla carefully closed the bathroom door. She'd left the light on, but stood at the door listening. Because she doubted either one could make sounds loud enough to be heard through the door, she sneaked a look inside and saw them wrestling with each other on the throw rug. The little male broke away from his sister and scampered to the litter pan to inspect it. The little girl followed and Marla quietly closed the door, relieved they were making themselves at home and didn't seem at all unhappy or distressed to be shut in the bathroom.

"So you haven't had a cat before," Jake said when they got back to the living room. It wasn't a question but the lead in to more on the subject.

"No. Should I worry?" she asked lightly, then watched his reaction. He didn't seem skeptical about her chances for success with the kittens, but he did seem faintly amused.

"You'll do fine. But when those two get their bellies full and start to feel secure, they're gonna to be into everything and always up to something."

Marla smiled. "I know at least that much about cats."

"Are you sure you want to keep them both?"

"Since they're brother and sister, they should stay together." The words came out stronger than she'd intended and Marla realized how vehement she sounded.

The kittens were more or less fraternal twins, just as she and Jaicey were. For some reason, she and her sister had been split up and adopted separately. Though it wasn't the same, Marla couldn't consider splitting up the kittens. Yes, she was aware litter mates almost always did go to separate homes and probably forgot about each other, but she didn't have the heart to do it. These two had been deprived of enough.

And how in the world would she be able to choose which kitten to keep and which one to give away? She'd fallen in love with them both the moment they'd looked up at her with that helpless, resigned look.

Jake spoke again, and it pleased her that he seemed to approve of her feelings.

"They'll have each other for companionship while you're at work, so they'll be happier. Cats aren't a lot of work unless you count shredded furniture and drapes, and denuded plants. You'll have to watch that they don't eat any. Some plants are toxic."

Marla glanced toward the few she had around the room, and made a mental note to find out which ones could be a threat as she picked up her handbag. "I thought at first that you didn't like cats."

"I like cats just fine," he told her as he opened the door.

Marla stepped into the hall ahead of him and suffered a warm charge of sensation when his big hand settled on the back of her waist. The memory of his tenderness with the kittens only heightened her response to his touch now, and there was no way she could ignore it.

They had a late lunch at a sports bar and restaurant, and both ordered the house hamburger with the special sauce. Because the lunch crowd had gone, they were served quickly. Marla was starving, a little amazed that her faded appetite had revived. She'd had to force herself to eat for weeks now.

While they ate, Jake told her about a few of the cats who'd lived at the main house at the ranch. Marla relaxed with him even more when his stories revealed his affection for the animals. She loved that before she realized it and brought herself up short. Love wasn't a word she could afford to assign to anything about Jake. When she found an opportunity to ask about how Jaicey was doing, Jake accepted the change in subject then suggested she go to the hospital with him before he took her back to the apartment.

Marla tried to keep her excitement over that to herself as she listened to Jake tell her that Jaicey had been pestering the doctors to go home, and it was beginning to look like they were almost ready to allow it. Being invited to the hospital by Jake certainly gave her a reason to have contact with her sister and she was thrilled. Had he let go of the last of his reservations about her?

And Jaicey had to be feeling better, so maybe she'd

be more comfortable with Marla this time. It could also be that Jaicey had finally started to remember her, or soon would, and Marla's anticipation began to grow.

By the time they finished eating and were on their way to the hospital, Marla was almost beside herself. The bonus was that Jake seemed to enjoy being with her, and it was almost as if he wanted to prolong their time together.

Marla tried to tell herself that this was no more than politeness, that she was either imagining it or he was being exceptionally personable this afternoon. Maybe it was because he'd had a hot, filling meal. Heaven knew he probably hadn't eaten since breakfast, and neither had she.

The biggest problem now was that it was harder to completely believe that she wasn't the kind of woman who appealed to him, not when his dark gaze had looked across the table at her so often with warmth and male interest. As it occasionally did on the way to the hospital now.

She needed to be careful. After watching him with the kittens and spending more time with him, Jake Craddock was more appealing to her than ever. Worse, he was all but blasting through the careful wall she'd built around her heart.

Before this, the attraction she'd felt had been because of his rugged good looks and the security and sense of family he represented. Now he was touching her heart, calling it to himself, subtly coaxing her closer despite the emotional danger. Getting to know and love Jaicey had started this, but that didn't mean she could afford to include Jake.

Marla realized she was brooding over this, brooding when she ought to be thinking about Jaicey. She managed to distract herself from thoughts about Jake, mentally planning what she might say to her sister, and offering a hasty prayer for success. Things had to go better this time. Surely they would.

CHAPTER EIGHT

WHEN they reached Jaicey's room, her latest visitors were just leaving. Marla tried to be patient when the two women stopped to chat with Jake for a few minutes. Jake introduced her to them, so Marla smiled and said something polite, though everything in her was focused on seeing Jaicey. Finally the women were on their way.

Jaicey was sitting in a wheelchair by the window, the leg of the chair extended to elevate her broken leg. Her arm was perched on a special tray that had been bolted to the arm of the chair. She looked worlds better than she had a month ago, and though she was pale and had lost weight, she looked more like the old Jaicey. Marla was thrilled when she saw the velvet patch teddy bear lying on the bed, occupying the pillow as if it was waiting for the next nap.

But the moment Jaicey's gaze swung their way and caught sight of her, a shadow crossed her face and her pretty blue eyes ricocheted to Jake, suggesting an aversion to Marla that struck her heart like a fist.

Oh, Jaicey, why are you so wary of me?

Marla simply couldn't fathom the reason for her sister's reaction, and it left her almost breathless with hurt. Jake walked over to Jaicey, then bent down and kissed her cheek before he lowered himself to a crouch beside the wheelchair.

Jealousy nettled deep. *She* should have been able to walk over to Jaicey like Jake had and given her a kiss or hug. She was Jaicey's real sister, and her twin.

The childishness of those thoughts shocked her and she quickly banished them, but a fresh sense of loss made her feel hollow inside. Frustration and the fear that she'd permanently lost her sister filled that hollowness, and she suddenly knew she couldn't stand by out of the way as she'd done last time. Though Marla wasn't one to demand attention, she was suddenly desperate to reconnect with Jaicey.

"You remember Marla Norris from a couple of weeks ago, don't you, baby?" Jake was saying.

Jaicey obligingly looked at Marla, who'd been standing a little away so she wouldn't feel crowded. At least Jaicey managed a small brief smile and a soft hello, which was better than before.

"Hello," Marla said back. When Jaicey started to look from her to Jake, she quickly added, "You look like you feel lots better than the last time I was here."

Jake motioned her into one of the visitors' chairs while he took the other. Marla sat down, her gaze still holding Jaicey's. This might be one of the few chances she'd get and she wanted to make the most of it.

"And I like what you've done with your hair," she added, striving to sound friendly and casual and interested. The short cut was new and obviously professional, and the clever style also concealed the surgical incision. "Did Coralee do it for you?"

Mentioning Coralee was a way to confirm that she'd been close enough to Jaicey to know that Coralee cut Jaicey's hair. At the mention of Coralee, Jaicey's light brows crinkled with curiosity.

"You know Coralee?"

Marla was thrilled they were having even this much of a conversation. "You introduced us, and she cuts my hair now. She did a fine job for you. That short style looks great."

Jaicey stared at her a few moments, studying her face as if she was trying to place her—as if she were on the verge of remembering—before she belatedly remarked, "It's too short. I hate it."

"It'll grow out," Marla said optimistically. "Your hair grows so fast." Marla was thrilled she'd held her sister's attention this long, but her knowledgeable remark about Jaicey's hair was one too many, and sent her gaze shooting to Jake. At least she'd got that far, and Marla couldn't help the excitement she felt.

Until Jaicey said in a soft, urgent voice, "I'm really tired, Jake. Could you call the nurse?"

Jake's surprise was obvious, as was his sudden concern. "Are you feelin' bad, darlin'?"

"Just tired," Jaicey said quickly. "Do you mind?"

Jake got up to reach the call button.

Marla was stricken, horrified by the impression that she'd been too pushy. That Jaicey would suddenly end a visit with Jake because of it sent fierce shame through her. She should have known better.

Jake moved his chair away to place it against the wall, so Marla stood and waited dazedly while Jake took her chair to place it beside the other one. She wasn't sure she could come up with a normal-sounding goodbye, but somehow she did.

"I'm sorry you're tired, Jaicey, but the rest is good for you. Have a good nap and get your strength back."

Marla tried to smile a little when Jaicey briefly glanced her way, but she felt too chastened to manage much of one before she turned to walk out of the room. Once in the hall, she stopped a few steps away from the door so she wouldn't be tempted to eavesdrop.

The natural way she and Jaicey had instantly liked each other and quickly bonded months ago was completely gone now—maybe forever—and her heart was heavy with grief. Jake was sure to have something to say about what had happened, and she dreaded that. It was certain there'd be no more invitations to visit Jaicey, which made things seem even more impossible.

Why hadn't she just kept silent and seen how Jake

would lead the conversation? He'd started things out well, but then she'd jumped in. What had she been thinking? That she'd get Jaicey to talk and once she did, that she'd remember everything?

The remorse she felt was suffocating. She'd been too eager. She'd apologize to Jake right away for spoiling his visit, and ask him to please convey her apologies to Jaicey.

A hot tear shot down her cheek and she jerked up a hand to dash it away, appalled. She'd always been able to will tears back, but suddenly her eyelids felt like pitiful dams against the ocean of tears that surged harder and higher with each heartbeat. Her body had gone rigid with the effort, but no more tears leaked out. Now all she had to do was face Jake, weather whatever he'd say, then endure the ride home.

The big hand that settled on her shoulder startled her, and she jerked, automatically flinching away from the touch as she glanced back. Jake's rugged face hardened in surprise, and his gaze searched hers sharply before it gentled.

"I didn't mean to startle you," he said quietly. "And I'm sorry about what happened in there. Jaicey's not herself."

Marla stared at him, caught completely off guard. She'd half expected him to descend on her like some avenging angel, but she hadn't dreamed *he'd* apologize to *her.*

That was the moment the day caught up with her. She could have dealt with Jake's anger. In fact, it would have helped shore up her emotions. Harshness from him would have deeply disturbed her, but she would have been able to face it stoically.

But she'd never developed strong defenses against kindness. The soft regret in Jake's dark eyes was so genuine that she felt the last of her control begin to unravel. Another hot tear shot down her cheek and she abruptly turned away to walk briskly toward the elevators, alarmed and terrified she'd break down completely. When had she become such a crybaby?

Jake not only fell into step beside her, his strong arm came around her waist to slow her down. She fitted naturally against his side from shoulder to knee, the heat of his body affecting her in a way that weakened her more. The elevator door opened on an empty car and they stepped inside.

Forced to give up any illusion of control, Marla opened her handbag and rummaged madly for a tissue. Once she had one, she pressed it tightly against her mouth, praying she could stifle the emotions that were about to crash through. Jake's arm tightened and she felt him lean close.

"What happened was my fault. I shouldn't have put you in that position in the first place."

He meant to be sympathetic, to take all the blame, but he was making things worse. As irrational as it was, his well-meaning words were not helping, and a hysterical little giggle burst up.

"I—I wish you'd stop being n-nice."

"Nice makes you cry, huh?" he said gruffly, his breath tickling her hot cheek. "You're either too proud to cry, or too stubborn, Miss Marlie. That's why you get the giggles."

Marla couldn't stifle another little gurgle at his gentle scolding, and sheer frustration—with herself and his dead-on remarks—rushed up to save her.

"You're supposed to look the other way and pretend not to notice."

"You want me to ignore a lady in distress?"

Oh, he was killing her! Though she couldn't make herself look at his face to see for sure, she felt compassion from him that was confirmed when his arm tightened comfortingly around her. Another desperate little tear streaked down her cheek accompanied by another excruciatingly embarrassing giggle.

"It would help if you'd stop being so gallant," she got out, a little shocked at the grouchy sound of her own voice.

"And now you're mad at me because I've witnessed that steely little spine and cool composure falter. So shoot me."

That surprised another little giggle out of her and another maddening tear, only this time she managed to reclaim her control by giving a hard, unladylike sniffle before she shoved the crumpled tissue back in her handbag.

The elevator opened on one of the hospital floors, and other passengers got on, relieving some of her tension and, she hoped, distracting Jake from zeroing in on her. He straightened a little, but he didn't take his arm away. The elevator only went down one more floor before it stopped again. She meant to pull away from him, but told herself it would be rude and maybe look too defensive. She'd shown Jake too much already, so she felt compelled to stay where she was.

The truth was, it felt good to have the comfort of a bigger, stronger body, and she liked the warmth that sluiced through her.

Then there was that last stop, that last boarding of visitors that packed them in so closely she had to slip her arm around his lean middle to make more room for others. His arm tightened in a way that turned her toward him a little more and she felt pleasure tingle over her skin.

The close contact continued as the car reached the main floor and they waited for it to empty. By that time her body had completely rebelled against her will and relaxed against him. When it was their turn to get off, Jake didn't loosen his arm much or take it away, and she couldn't seem to drop her arm from around his waist.

Forget about *trying* to be Jake's "friend." There was no try to it. They were suddenly a man and woman who fit perfectly together, strolling off the elevator and through the lobby as if they were a couple of long stand-

ing who did this all the time. Marla was a little stunned
that she felt so at ease.

She realized then that she didn't feel so shaken and
upset. The heartbreak and desperation that had overwhelmed her after seeing Jaicey was completely
soothed. The fact that it had been Jake's embrace and
the wonderful sense of security he gave her that had
done it was something she had to be on guard against.

And yet she couldn't seem to muster much of a de-
fense. She didn't feel self-conscious at all about having
her arm around him or having so much of her body
touching his. She'd always been overly aware of even
the smallest physical contact with others, and almost always felt awkward about it, so this was a kind of miracle for her. A miracle, but a miracle she had to find the
strength to reject. The reminder caused an instant burst
of rebellion.

Why did she always have to be so independent, so
fearful? Why couldn't she accept this now without
qualms and without future expectations, just enjoying
it while it lasted then walking peacefully away when it
was over?

She'd always been too needy, that's why. And this
man was already claiming more of her heart than she
should have allowed. The idea that she couldn't trust
herself anymore wasn't as jarring as it should have been,
and for the first time she wondered if there was even a
tiny chance that it might be safe to care about a man,

that just once it might be safe to lean a little on someone else, to see how things might go if she took a modest chance.

No doubt she'd agonize over the hazards once she got home and Jake was gone, but was she really risking so much? What was a little friendship between a man and a woman? That was all that was realistically possible anyway.

By the time they reached the pickup, Marla was weary of trying to talk her heart into friendship and away from the tantalizing notion of something deeper. If Jake had been any other man she'd ever met, she would have succeeded almost right away.

As he helped her into the tall vehicle, their gazes met and clung for a long moment before she forced herself to look away. The intensity in his eyes had made her feel even more exposed to him, but the gleam she'd seen for that little heartbeat of time had been an arresting mix of curiosity, understanding and male intent.

He was figuring things out. Not the things between her and Jaicey or anything to do with their secret, but he was figuring *her* out. It was a surprise that a tiny part of her wanted him to, a tiny part that wanted him to know everything about her. But mostly, she was scared of that, terrified of being found out then rejected by the man she admired and was so deeply attracted to.

She thought instead about Jaicey. The mystery of why Jaicey was so leery of her was one she had to solve, and it relieved her to fixate on that. She couldn't give up on her sister, couldn't allow another person she loved to be taken from her. She wasn't a powerless child at the mercy of others anymore. She could fight for Jaicey. However it might end up, Marla couldn't just let her go.

Because it wasn't long now until they got to her apartment, and Jake—hopefully—went on home, she spoke up when he stopped the pickup for a red light.

"After I went out of the room, did Jaicey mention what it is about me that upsets her?" Jake glanced over at her.

"She's not taking the memory loss well, and she's not ready to deal with it." His dark gaze searched hers. "I hope you'll make allowances for her. The minute you were out the door, she felt bad and said so."

He reached across the seat and put his hand over the back of hers.

"Give her time. She was born curious. Once she feels better and more able to take on the world again, she'll have to know all about you, if she hasn't remembered on her own by then."

His fingers closed reassuringly around hers and Marla couldn't help a fresh surge of feeling for him. Her heart was suddenly in her throat. The reassurance he'd given her, combined with the low, sexy timbre of his voice, was almost impossible to withstand. Somehow, she pulled her hand from his and looked away to begin searching through her handbag as if there was some-thing in there she had to have this very moment.

"The k-kittens," she babbled. "I almost forgot. They'll be starved by now."

Her voice had wavered as she'd said that, but to her relief the light changed and Jake drove through the intersection without appearing to notice. He was watching the street ahead, not her, so she relaxed a little.

Now that she had her keys in hand, she'd be ready to get out of the truck the instant they got to her apartment. Jake would surely go on home, and she could take care of the babies and recover from the day. It helped that she was going home to a pair of kittens, and for the first time she realized how good it felt to be going home to someone.

Some*ones,* she amended, and her heart lifted a little. She had a pair of little someones now to take care of and enjoy, harmless, nonthreatening little creatures to keep her company and, if they were like other kittens she'd seen, to make her laugh and fill in a few lonely places in her life. It was safe to love them.

Of course, they were no substitute for Jaicey—no one could be that—but they'd take her mind off herself and her problems with her sister. And the problem of her growing feelings for Jake.

CHAPTER NINE

JAKE hinted that he wasn't quite ready to end their day together, and Marla tried not to feel flattered. He'd asked to see how the kittens were doing, and since he'd helped rescue them, *and* her, and tried to get them off to a good start, she couldn't say no. Truth to tell, she'd liked watching him with the kittens. It had healed something in her to see that, and she wouldn't mind seeing it again.

After the babies were fed, Jake put them on the carpet with a small ball, and they were looking it over. As Marla got up to take the lids to the kitchen and rinse them off, Jake nudged the ball with the toe of his boot to make it roll and the kittens chased after it. They were losing their shyness, and Marla felt good about that.

When she came back into the living room, Jake nudged the ball again and the kittens scrambled. She stopped where she was because the ball was rolling toward her. Once they'd caught it, Jake walked closer to pick it up to make it bounce away. The kittens watched, their little heads tilting up and down as they watched it then gave chase.

"Have you thought up names yet?" Jake asked.

"I haven't had much time to think about it."

"Cats learn their names pretty quick. Of course, they'll pretend to ignore them when it suits them. That's one of the challenges with cats."

Marla shook her head as she watched them bat the ball and try to take a bite of it when it stopped.

"When you look into those sweet little faces, it's hard to think they'd ever be a challenge," she said, meaning that.

Jake chuckled and turned to her. They were both standing in the middle of the living room floor. Marla tried not to step back as he reached for her hands and held them between them.

"Tell me that in a few weeks or months," he said, his dark eyes twinkling down at her. "They'll love you, though, however fickle and finicky they'll act from time to time. They just won't show it as constantly as a dog does."

It touched her that Jake thought the kittens would love her. Or maybe he was just speaking generally about cats and their owners, and she'd taken it too personally. It was hard not to take it personally, though, especially when he was holding her hands and rubbing his thumbs gently over their backs.

Then he added, "They're too proud to act dependent."

She knew right away that he wasn't talking about cats in general, but that he'd figured out she had an aversion to being dependent and to showing it. After their visit with Jaicey when she'd been so upset, that wasn't surprising.

"That's hardly a character flaw."

He gave her a slow smile. "You're like a cat. Proud, independent. One minute you're soft and vulnerable, the next you're aloof and hard to get close to."

His gaze was alive with male interest. Marla felt his fingers tighten the tiniest bit and glanced away, rattled by the wild cascade of fear and excitement that stormed through her.

"Would you like coffee now?" she asked stiffly, then felt her face go hot as she heard the frost in her voice.

"No, thanks, I don't want more coffee just now, Marlie," he said, chuckling again as if he was delighted she'd unintentionally proved his point. "You don't mind if I call you Marlie once in a while, do you?"

"It's okay." Her voice was a half-whisper, and some strange magnetism between them made her gaze slip back up to his.

Jake's smile turned sexy and the air began to thicken. He was going to kiss her. He leaned toward her and she watched, transfixed, unbelieving, as his eyes dropped shut the second before his lips made gentle contact with hers. Her lashes fluttered for a few panicked seconds, then closed.

The tender kiss was persuasive. Whatever she'd

thought Jake's lips might feel like, it was nothing compared to this, warm, firm, caressing. He released her hands and his arms came around her, but his lips stayed gentle, coaxing. She belatedly thought about pulling away—there was still time to keep this brief!—but it was at that moment that his lips surged hotly against hers, and he pulled her against him so tightly she could feel both their heartbeats.

There was no other place for her hands to go but up his chest to his shoulders then slowly, as he deepened the kiss, her will evaporated and her hands slipped helplessly around his neck. Male experience and desire intensified the power of his tender and relentless advance, and all Marla could do was hope to survive the hot whirlwind of sensuality it unleashed in her.

Her legs had stopped supporting her the moment the kiss had changed, and though she tried to hold him tightly to stay upright, her body felt so limp that even her arms felt weak. Her head was spinning. She was so dominated by the clamor of female desire and the delicious things his kiss was doing to her, that she couldn't think.

The kiss seemed to go on and on, and she was greedy for it. The sense of devouring as she was being devoured reached a fever pitch before the kiss suddenly ended. Her lashes spasmed open and her sharp gasp for air brought back enough sense to her brain to make her realize that Jake was dragging in air, and that his big body was trembling.

For the first time in her life, Marla felt powerful. A feminine confidence she'd never had before rose up. Jake had kissed her, and now he was out of breath. Jake Craddock, macho tough guy, was now trembling in her arms like one of the kittens!

It didn't matter that she was just as out of breath as he was and just as shaken. She'd never known what real desire was until his kiss had brought it to life in her. No doubt, it was a feeling he was very familiar with, but it was a compliment that he seemed to be feeling it now.

For her! He made her feel like the most potent and desirable female in the world.

Though she knew a man like him could easily make any woman feel like this, right now, right at this moment, *she* was that woman. *She* was the one he was focused on now, *she* was the one he'd kissed. Her heart was going wild over that, but her shocked brain was laboring to bring her back to earth, or to at least give her some contact with reality.

But she didn't want reality, she wanted Jake. As her body began to settle down, it became easier for her brain to reassert common sense.

It wasn't completely successful at first. Instead Marla was thinking about the fact that Jake had surely kissed more than his share of women. After all, a man like him could have any woman he wanted and, as far as she knew, there was no one he was serious about right now...

Her heart ran with that idea for a few moments until

the bitter plume of truth began to tinge that sweet and foolish rush of excitement: No one made commitments to her that they kept.

It was as if her heart had stopped beating for a moment as the brutal reminder came at her full force. She'd been thirteen when she'd come to believe that she wasn't the kind of person people kept. That's when she'd finally given up on permanency, and she'd learned to rely only on herself for the things she needed.

When Jake had gotten enough insight to compare her to a cat, he might also have gotten enough insight to know that she was the kind of person he'd never need to make any sort of commitment to. He probably viewed her catlike independence as a lucky thing, so why not kiss her?

A chill went through her. Losing people had never been a choice she'd made, those decisions had all been made for her. For whatever reason Jake had spent time with her today, however he'd made her feel, she had to remember that there was nothing permanent about this. Jake probably knew that better than she did.

That's why he could kiss her like there was no tomorrow. Because there would be no tomorrow. He'd have absolute faith in that because he'd be the one to make it come true.

The chill deepened, and she made a restless move that prompted Jake to lift his head. He was looking down at her in a new way now. A handful of seconds ago, she would have been flattered. His eyes were still heavy-lidded with desire, his face still harsh with it, and he was staring down at her as if he meant to kiss her again. Her brain searched desperately for a way to avoid another kiss, and remembered the babies.

"Oh!" She pulled back and glanced around the floor. "The kittens!"

She hated that she sounded as breathless as she felt, but Jake loosened his arms and she slipped away. The kittens were nowhere in sight, and she thanked heaven that they'd given her an excuse to escape Jake and perhaps spend enough time chasing them down to completely put an end to what he'd started.

As she walked around the room, searching, she could feel his gaze on her. Could he tell she was using the kittens to cool things off, or would he think she was just being responsible? On the other hand, he had a male ego. Maybe her ability to even think of the kittens after that searing kiss would offend him.

She preferred that last possibility, because it would save some of her pride if he thought she could walk away from him after a kiss like that, particularly when he might have been about to start a second one. The fact that the kittens weren't in the living room or the kitchen was enough of a real concern to bring her completely back to earth. Where were they?

She heard Jake's bootsteps behind her as she walked down the hall and checked the bathroom. When she didn't find them there, she realized they might have gone on to the sewing room and she felt a nettle of alarm. There were all kinds of things in there that might hurt them, the biggest being stray pins or needles. Or bits of thread or beads they might eat.

She rushed in to turn on the light to search every place kittens that small might hide. She was aware Jake had reached around the corner into her bedroom across the hall and switched on the light, though he hadn't gone in.

"They're in here," he called, and she turned to rush to the hall.

To her surprise, Jake acted as if her bedroom was off-limits, and it pleased her that he didn't seem to think he was entitled to just walk in, not even for the kittens.

"The second I turned on the light, they ran like roaches," he said with a chuckle. "One went into your closet. Do you want me to round up the other one?"

"Yes, go ahead."

Marla didn't think about anything but going after the kitten in the closet or she would have remembered the large, framed photograph of her and Jaicey.

The smaller one—the girl—had ducked into a shoe, and peeked out at her playfully. Marla laughed and picked up the kitten-stuffed shoe, then turned to show Jake.

Jake stood by her dresser watching her, the male kitten already captured and looking around the room from his high perch. Jake looked solemn but she'd already held out the shoe to show him the kitten.

That's when she remembered she'd leaned the matted picture frame on the floor against the side of her dresser. Her gaze shot to where it sat, but it was facing the dresser on the side opposite the one Jake was standing beside. He couldn't have seen it.

"Doesn't she look sweet?" she asked, recovering.

"She does. You've got a beautiful laugh, Marlie," he said somberly. "I realized just now that I've never heard it before, not lighthearted like that. You're beautiful when you laugh."

Marla lowered the shoe, then looked down to gently take the kitten out as she tried not to let herself be seduced by such a lavish compliment. And she thought about that kiss. The way she'd kissed him back might have given him a green light to try for more. He was an experienced, red-blooded male, and she couldn't ignore that they were standing in her bedroom.

But it wouldn't mean a thing to him. It would last while it lasted, then he'd go away. And even if he didn't go right away, he would sometime. And she'd never get over it. She summoned every scrap of levelheaded sense she had.

"Nice try, cowboy."

Now a smile sneaked over his handsome mouth and he drawled out a low, "But I wasn't trying to seduce you. Not yet."

Not yet. Marla felt the shock—and the promise—of that go deep. A wave of weakness, just like when he'd kissed her, swept through her. As casually as she could, she turned toward the closet and tossed the empty shoe inside before she started for the hall. Jake followed at a leisurely pace.

"You are beautiful when you laugh," he went on, obviously not finished with the subject. "I admit the timing made it sound suspicious, considering where we were when I heard you laugh and saw your face, but it's true."

They reached the living room. Marla set her kitten on the carpet, so Jake did the same with the one he had before he straightened. Marla clasped her hands together in front of her, hoping he'd keep his distance. At least they were standing near the door, but she'd tried to arrange it that way. She could still feel that wonderful and frightening pull between them, and had real worries about being exposed to it much longer.

"You're beautiful all the time, Marlie," he said, solemn again, "but when you laugh like that, it changes you. The shadows go away and your eyes go bright."

A blush came to her cheeks, and she felt a self-conscious giggle bubble up. She barely managed to keep it back, though she felt the reluctant smile on her lips. "Thank you for the compliment, but if you don't mind, it's been a really long day."

"It has been," he agreed, giving her the same sexy smile that rocked her every time she saw it.

It relieved her when he reached for his Stetson on the entry table. But then he stood just holding it.

"Would you let me pick you up in the morning? Take you to the ranch for the day? You could bring the kittens along and they could stay at the house. That way, they won't feel abandoned and you can keep them on a feeding schedule."

Marla's heart leaped. Jaicey would still be in the hospital, so this invitation was strictly Jake's idea. And from the look in his eyes, it was something he wanted very much.

It was hard not to take this to heart, *so hard,* but she had to. She'd never forget that kiss, and she'd never forget the way Jake made her feel, especially today. She couldn't spend another day, just with him.

If she did, he'd expect to find out more about her from here on, and he'd be right to. After all, part of what went on between a man and a woman who were seeing each other included sharing their history, sharing confidences, and she couldn't share much. She hadn't even told Jaicey a lot, because the little she'd told her had upset her, and Jaicey had felt guilty for having it so good.

She just couldn't spend any more time with Jake, especially after that kiss, but her heart protested that. Heavens, a day at the ranch didn't mean he had plans to marry her! This was a simple invitation to a nice time. She didn't have to blab every detail of her life to allow herself a little enjoyment, perhaps a few kisses, and the fun of going to the ranch again.

She remembered Jaicey's secret, but her heart insisted that Jaicey's secret was hers, hers to keep, hers to tell…hers to remember.

But then common sense chimed in with a swift review of all the reasons she needed to put an end to this, until her nerves were screaming with the stress of wanting to be with Jake and knowing she shouldn't.

Several moments had ticked by while she'd hesitated. She still couldn't make up her mind, torn between the idea that she suddenly couldn't bear to turn him down, and the idea that letting things go farther between them was dangerous.

Sanity made a last common sense bid and she opened her mouth to decline, but instead she heard herself say, "I'd like that."

It took another of Jake's sexy smiles to make her realize she really hadn't turned him down, but the frantic feeling she expected didn't come.

"What time?" he asked. "Would seven be too early?"

Marla suddenly realized how long a day at the ranch could be if her time with him started at 7:00 a.m.

"H-how about I drive myself to the ranch?" she asked. "I'm really overdue to get my car out on the highway." Jake took it well, but she could see the sudden alertness in his eyes, the curiosity.

"You can do whatever you like, Miss Marla. I really do hope you'll be able to spend the day, but you can get there however you want, then leave whenever you like."

Marla felt a little ashamed of herself, and guilty. "It

wouldn't offend you?" He smiled again, a gentle smile that told her he was amused instead of offended.

"You worry too much, darlin'. I'll see you in the morning at seven, however you want to get there. Let me know if you want me to pick you up, and don't forget your kittens."

"Are you sure they wouldn't be better off here instead, with plenty of food? I'll be at work all day again on Monday."

"They'll be fine either way."

"All right," she said, and to her relief, he turned to open the hall door.

"Thank you for the invitation," she said as he glanced back at her. "And thanks again for everything today."

One corner of his mouth quirked up. "My pleasure. Good night." And then he was out the door.

Marla lifted her hands to her face and pressed her fingers to her hot cheeks. She'd crossed a personal line just now, and though she felt a small amount of panic, there was something about today and the idea of going to the ranch tomorrow that felt right. It was as if she'd caught a hint of something wonderful, something so tantalizing she just had to have a closer look.

Was it Jake or was it because she realized she felt a little freer? Something about today had changed something in her, made her feel a little braver, a little more secure. Maybe that's why she'd not been able to turn him down. Maybe she wanted to see where this change would lead, or find some way to build on it.

Maybe she was feeling a little braver and a little more secure because Jake had seemed to understand her quirks, including the one about driving herself when she was uncertain or needed to know there was an avenue of easy escape. He'd seemed to understand a lot about her today, but when she considered it, she realized she wasn't surprised.

Jake was the brother Jaicey practically idolized, so of course he'd be a cut above other men, and as a good brother, he might be more sensitive to female feelings. Jaicey had a plethora of feelings, so he'd had plenty of experience.

He'd been sensitive enough to realize how upset she was, both this morning and at the hospital. When she'd grabbed his arm at the ditch, he'd seen her terror, but he hadn't catered to it. She realized she trusted him more than if he'd suddenly gone sympathetic, because not all sympathy men showed was genuine. Jake had simply gone about his business, finding the kittens, searching for more, lecturing her, but despite all that male bluster, he'd demonstrated he wasn't a danger to her or the kittens.

After she'd seen Jaicey that afternoon, he'd understood that upset too, and from the things he'd said, he'd understood her almost too well. The memory of the comfort he'd given moved over her like a warm wave.

Jake had guessed a lot about her today, and probably even guessed a few things about why she was so on guard with others and why she was so reserved. The fact that he still wanted to see her again tomorrow, sent her fears almost completely away.

If she was wrong about him, she was wrong. Her pride had been dented before and her feelings had been hurt. She'd been disillusioned lots of times, so it wasn't as if she didn't know how to survive it. It dawned on her more fully then that she'd rather take a risk on Jake and have things go wrong, than to miss out on the possibility that he truly was that one man she might have a chance with.

A tickle on the top of her foot made her look down to see the female kitten plucking at the toe strap of her sandal, while the male kitten was batting at his sister's tail.

Marla smiled as she bent down and picked them up. They wiggled, apparently not ready to cuddle, so she found the feathered wand and carried the babies over to the sofa and sat down. They played with the feather for several minutes before the male set off to explore the sofa cushions and try to climb up the sofa back. The female followed.

Marla set the feathered wand aside, and thought about the visit to the ranch Jaicey had planned all those weeks ago. The wreck had spoiled those plans, but Marla thought about finding at least one arrowhead and maybe seeing a cougar track and following it. She wondered if anyone had taken the time these past weeks to track the cougar, and if they'd ever found it.

After a few minutes, the kittens found their way back to her lap and settled together there. Marla realized how grateful she was to have found a couple of little friends, friends who needed her and wouldn't care who she was or what she did as long as she was good to them.

Marla picked them up and gave each of them a little kiss on the head. They squirmed over the kisses, as if they were worried she might bite them or eat them, which made her smile.

"You're always going to be safe, little ones. No more hunger, no more cold nights—if you've had any yet— no more blistering days, and no more fear, I promise."

Marla cuddled them close, realizing that her heart felt light, and she was excited about seeing Jake again tomorrow. Eventually she reached for her TV remote to see the news and hear how hot it was expected to be.

CHAPTER TEN

As HE drove home to the ranch, Jake realized that was the second time Marla had put a sudden end to his visit, and he was amused. The night after the wreck, she'd rushed him out the door because he was holding her hand and she'd sensed he might kiss her. Tonight, it had taken her longer to put an end to things, but she'd managed to make it clear that his time was up.

That kiss had obviously shaken her, which was fine with him because it had shaken him up, too. He'd never forget it. Her response had all but taken him apart, and yet it hadn't been because she was very experienced, because he could tell she wasn't.

Most men shied away from women who were as aloof and complicated as she was, so it was no surprise that she might never have been kissed like that. And she was so reserved, so proper in her manner, that he'd bet there were a lot of men who wouldn't have tried to in the first place.

She was the kind of woman you didn't fool around

with unless you meant business, but that didn't trouble him. In fact, the idea appealed to him. He'd been attracted to her from the moment he'd seen her, and he'd felt the instant chemistry. It had managed to intensify his misgivings about her sudden friendship with Jaicey, but he'd changed his mind since then.

Marlie was a sweet woman, shy, yet able to stand up for herself. He liked that she was no-nonsense. She'd tried to save a pair of grungy kittens, because she hadn't had the heart to leave them to starve or get killed. Then she'd refused to let them be separated, and had been willing to spend a chunk of money to get them vet care, and far more at the pet store than they needed to survive. She had a good heart and maybe a generous one.

She'd also refused to let him cover the costs. The message that she wouldn't take advantage of him, not even over an amount that meant nothing to him, made it clear she didn't care how much money the Craddocks had, she didn't feel entitled to have any of it come her way.

And she'd handled those kittens as if they were as fragile as butterflies. It was easy to see they'd be safe with her, that anything small or dependent would be safe with her and well cared for, and that spoke volumes to him.

The memory of how she handled the kittens reminded him of the touch of her elegant hands, and he felt a fresh rush of desire. She was a woman whose every movement drew the eye, and he thought about that for a few miles before his mind turned to more practical things, especially the mystery he'd sensed from the first.

He didn't know a thing about the family she and Jaicey said lived around here, but he was beginning to suspect there was something sad about Marla's upbringing. There had to be a reason for her to be so cautious about people, and the fact that she had defenses galore.

She didn't like to show strong emotion, even when it would have been understandable to let it show, like today at the hospital when she'd done everything but stand on her head to keep from crying in front of him. That aversion to showing emotion was sometimes a clue that someone had suffered some kind of abuse as a child, or had been severely and repeatedly reprimanded for it.

Which reminded him of this morning at the ditch, when he'd been angry and she'd been terrified he was out of control and would hurt the kittens. She'd shocked him to his toes.

*Please—don't hurt them! They're so tiny and afraid!...
Please don't take it out on them!*

She'd had a hold on his arm that declared she was prepared to drag him back to the road if she'd had to in order to save those kittens from him. It hadn't mattered that her size and his made that impossible; she would have tried for all she was worth.

He'd been grouchy because she'd risked real danger to herself, but he'd never in his life harmed or treated little animals roughly. She'd offended the hell out of him before he'd seen the terrified look in her eyes and realized her fear was genuine.

It had made a deep impression on him, deeper still as time had gone on. Miss Marlie had secrets, maybe hurtful ones, and her pride might resist disclosing them. If she'd been abused, then there might also be secrets she'd be too ashamed to reveal. She was a proud woman overall, but it was the kind of pride that loathed showing weakness. There was usually a reason for that, too.

But from time to time today, she'd let down some of her defenses. His favorite had been when she'd laughed at the kitten in her shoe. For a few moments he believed he'd glimpsed a carefree side of her that might not have had much encouragement to show itself.

He'd suddenly wanted to do that, encourage more of that fun-loving side of her, to make her laugh and chase the shadows away. No other woman had ever inspired that kind of thing in him, so he paid attention to it.

He thought about what she might enjoy doing tomorrow, and began to make a few plans.

Judd heard his son come in from the back and down the short east hall toward the den. He closed the ruined photo album, slid it into a leather satchel behind the desk, then settled back in the swivel chair just as Jake stopped in the door frame.

"Where's Miss Connie tonight?" Jake asked.

"Out with the girls. How come you aren't out paintin' the town?"

"Painted it today," Jake said with a badly suppressed grin.

"Miss Marla doesn't impress me as a gal who paints the town," Judd commented. "I hear the two of you were up to see Jaicey today."

"We were. It didn't last long."

"I heard that, too." Judd leaned back farther in the swivel chair. "You might as well come on in and sit down."

Jake obliged and walked over to sit at the end of the sofa nearest the big desk. When he stretched out his long legs, his boot brushed against the warped and banged up briefcase from Jaicey's wrecked car.

Jaicey had asked them yesterday about the things that had been in her car, and had asked daddy to bring her anything he thought she needed to see before she got home. When Judd had mentioned the briefcase to her, Jaicey had been surprised. She hadn't been able to think of a reason for it to have been in her car.

Jake nodded toward the case. "I see you got it open."

"Almost had to take a hacksaw to it," Judd remarked, but didn't offer any comment on what he'd found inside.

"What else did you do today?" Jake asked, not particularly interested in the contents of the briefcase, other than the fact that it belonged to his sister and she could carry what she wanted in it.

"This 'n' that. What do you know about Miss Marla?"

Jake smiled a little at his father's change of subject. He wasn't shy when he wanted to know something.

"Not nearly enough yet. You already know she's not

the kind who talks about herself, or has to be the center of attention. She reminds me of Grandma Luz, with her quilts and needlework. I told you she was the one who made that bear for Jaicey, and you should see her sewing room. She'd probably like to see grandma's things in the attic and the quilts on loan to the county museum."

Judd's brows had gone up. "Sounds to me like you did spend a lot of time with her today. You hardly ever talk so much about a woman. And how'd that happen? You didn't say anything about her at breakfast."

Jake wasn't used to his father being this inquisitive about a woman he was seeing. And Jake wasn't seeing Marla regularly, though he expected that to change. He hoped it would. "We crossed paths this morning, and that kept leading to other things until the whole day was filled up."

"Has she ever mentioned she's adopted?"

Jake all but did a double-take at the surprising question. "Adopted?"

"So I reckon she hasn't," Judd concluded. "Ever find out about that family Jaicey said was living nearby? Ever meet any?"

"I don't know a thing. None of the Norrises in the area ever heard of her." Now Jake was wary. Though his father had been able to tell things had changed between him and Marla, his questions were pointed and becoming a little relentless. And what made Judd think Marla had been adopted?

"Then it sounds like you've still got a lot to find out about her," Judd said with bluntness of a man believed in plain talk. "I assume from the look on your face when you swaggered in here, that she made quite an impression on you today. Am I right?"

"Right as rain so far." Jake shook his head a little at his father's accurate assessment. That's what this was about. Judd wanted to know about a woman Jake seemed interested in. "I invited her out here tomorrow. Any objections?"

"Not a one. I might steal her away for a while myself."

"Oh, yeah?"

"Why not? She's managed to befriend Jaicey and now she's put a gleam in your eye. Not all Jaicey's curiosity came from genetics, you know. She got at least some of it from me."

"You've been around Marla before," Jake pointed out.

"And I liked her, liked her a lot," Judd said.

Jake thought nothing of his father using past tense. Judd swiveled the desk chair to the side, leaned down, then stood up with the strap of his old leather satchel in his hand.

"'Bout time for me to turn in," Judd said as he came around the desk and walked toward the door. "Night, son."

Jake watched as he walked past. "Night."

He stayed up a while after that, wondering what was on his father's mind. Something was, but it was a waste of breath to ask. Judd would talk once he was good and ready. Jake smiled at the familiar trait, then stood to reach for Jaicey's battered and warped briefcase.

It was empty, but he closed it as far as it would go, then carried it to one of the low cabinets at the side of the room to leave it there.

He had a thought about his father asking if Marla had mentioned she was adopted, but he didn't give that question a lot of significance. Maybe he'd been wondering what Marla had in common with Jaicey that had made them such fast friends. He'd wondered, too, but he hadn't given adoption a thought.

Jake made a pass through the house to switch off the lights, then went on up to bed himself.

Marla got to the ranch just before 7:00 a.m. and parked her car in a shady part of the front driveway. She'd dressed in a long-sleeved, blue plaid cotton shirt and jeans. Though she'd brought along sandals and a pair of athletic shoes, she was wearing her Western boots.

She carried her Stetson. She wasn't used to wearing it around like Jaicey and several of the ranch women in the area did, but she was from the city. Everyone knew she was, so it felt pretentious to wear it unless she planned to be out in the sun.

Overall, Marla was excited to be here, excited about the day. Though it was already hot, there was something refreshing about being at the ranch. The size of everything was intimidating, but she liked it. The size of

Chicago was overwhelming, too, but it wasn't half as appealing to her anymore.

There was a wonderful sense of freedom all the way out here, and Marla felt it strongly this morning. She liked the sound of the birds, liked watching them at the large birdbath in front of the house as she walked to the door. She liked the clean air—even when it was filled with dust or animal smells—because it was natural and smog-free. She especially liked the smell of hay and leather.

Being here lifted her heart. The only thing that made it less than it could have been was that Jaicey wasn't here. And then there was Jaicey's secret. Though it felt disloyal, Marla had wondered more than once since last night if there'd be an opportunity today to at least hint to Jake about it.

It had occurred to her that if the conditions were right and the opportunity presented itself, she could mention a couple of things about herself to Jake, then ask him to mention them to Jaicey. She wouldn't exactly be telling the secret herself, but maybe Jaicey's memory would be triggered, and she'd at least tell Jake about what she'd done and who Marla really was. Then the two of them could decide when and how to tell their father.

At the very least, there'd be no important secrets between her and Jake. Marla had realized late last night that if Jake could know Jaicey's secret and accept it, then she'd feel lots better about whatever more was possible between them.

Yes, it was selfish to think about herself, but she was also thinking about how Jake would feel about spending time with her once he found out she'd been keeping something so big from him. She wasn't the only one who had pride.

And she had a little confidence now. He hadn't dropped her cold over what she'd done at the ditch, and her upset at the hospital hadn't fazed him. He'd stretched out the day far longer than he'd had to yesterday. She'd given him more than one chance to leave, but he hadn't. And he'd kissed her. Then he'd let her know that one day together wasn't enough for him.

He'd made her feel as if she'd mattered, and as the hours had gone by after he'd left her apartment last night, she realized how novel that was in her life. Her view of herself and the world had become a little more optimistic, and she was able to see a few things a little differently. She doubted Jake had any idea what he'd done, but that didn't seem to matter to the result.

When she'd got up this morning, she'd realized she'd been a fool not to expect more from life than she had, a fool to be afraid she'd get her heart broken. What could be worse than keeping everyone at arm's length and believing no one would ever care about her enough to stay in her life? How could she know that, when she'd rarely given anyone a chance?

She was willing to take a chance today, and she wasn't as leery of that as she'd expected to be. Yesterday, she'd realized she couldn't just give up on Jaicey. By this morning she'd realized she had to stop giving up on herself.

Whatever happened, she'd deal with it. If she got hurt, so what? Hearts were risked and got broken every day. What was so fragile about hers that made her so obsessively protective of it?

Yesterday, she'd thought about Tommy. They'd lived a nightmare during their placement together, but she'd protected him and one day she'd found the courage to literally carry him out of the house, get on a bus and take him to a hospital. She'd been ten and he'd been two, and they'd both had enough bruises and marks to demonstrate the abuse to them both.

That had ended their time with that couple. She hadn't fared much better at her next home, but Tommy had been placed with a pastor and his wife, who'd later adopted him. She'd made that happen because she'd finally faced her fear and dared to do something that had rescued them both.

That's why she'd had the flashback about Tommy at the ditch. Not only because the situation had triggered the old memory and she'd mistaken Jake's anger for a monster's, but because there was something else her heart had wanted her to see about herself, something good.

And she'd had more courage at ten than she'd had since, but no more. Today was a new day, and she'd do her best to keep it as fresh and full of promise as it felt right now.

Marla stopped just before she reached the front door of the big ranch house and turned to take in a panoramic view of the land between the house and the highway. She inhaled the country air, drinking it in, feeling the life and energy it fueled.

Behind her the door opened, and she turned as Judd stepped out. He took her hand and moved close to bend down and give her a hug. Marla felt his easy strength and when she drew away, she noticed more than ever how much Jake looked like his father in coloring and physique. Judd was leaner and less muscular, but he was strong. It was hard to believe he had health problems of any kind.

"Glad to have you come out today, Miss Marla," he said. "Jake got called down to the barns. He said you could either wait for him to get back, or have me show you where he's at."

Marla shook her head, not wanting to offend when the choice was to spend time with Judd or with Jake. "Is this a trick question?"

Judd grinned down at her as if he approved of her answer. "Ah, you don't want to spend time with an old man when you could be with Jake, do you?"

She was saved from an answer when Miss Jenny called for him. "Telephone!"

He waved Marla inside ahead of him. "Make yourself at home, Miss Marla. I'll get rid of 'em quick."

Judd left her in the big living room, and Marla looked around. She'd been sitting long enough during the ride out here, so she walked over to look at the family pictures that virtually covered one of the walls from floor to ceiling in generational groupings, almost like mosaics. She loved those.

Each tintype, painting and photograph had been cleverly copied in one of three reduced sizes that gave the display harmony and protected the originals from exposure. Marla focused on some of the small paintings and tintypes from the 1800s, which included the first Craddocks, along with three Confederate soldiers from the Civil War era, who'd fought for the South. Then she looked at pictures of Craddocks who'd come after, and an occasional wedding photo. There were also photos and small copies of paintings that featured a few of the most memorable bulls and horses that had been acquired or bred on Craddock ranch.

Finally Marla got to the last two generations of Craddocks, and since she already had her own copies of Jaicey's pictures, she spent time now looking at early photos of Jake, both as an infant and a small boy, including ones of him with Jaicey and their mother, Lona. Jake had been a handsome, rough and tumble boy, and Marla suddenly had a mental picture of what his sons would look like. Maybe he'd have a dark-haired daughter or two, with dark eyes...

That's when Marla thought about Jaicey, and realized it was no wonder Jaicey had been curious about her birth family. She'd grown up in a house rich with family history, with a lot of that history displayed on this wall where she'd seen it day in and day out.

It seemed strange to her now that Jaicey had been so worried about telling her father and brother about the family search she'd gone on. Surely they, of all people, would have understood Jaicey's need to know something about her birth family. And Marla had seen this wall before herself. It amazed her now to realize how quickly she'd gone along with Jaicey's wishes about not confessing to Judd and Jake what she'd done. Of course, Jaicey knew her father and brother much better than she did, but it still seemed too much to expect that an adopted child wouldn't become curious about her birth family sooner or later.

Marla began to wonder if this wall could provide her with an opening of some kind to bring up the subject of Jaicey's birth family to Jake. She'd planned to only mention a couple of things that Jake could repeat to Jaicey that might prompt her to remember, but now that she was looking at this wall, she wondered if it might be possible to say something a little more directly to Jake. Maybe think of a hypothetical question or two to at least sound him out a little about how he thought his father might react, or how he might react.

Doing that could mean that she'd all but give the secret away, and that wouldn't be fair to Jaicey. Though Marla suddenly had doubts about how risky Jaicey's secret was, it still wasn't her secret to tell. Yes, she was just as caught up in it now as Jaicey was, but

Jake and Judd were Jaicey's family, not hers. It had been Jaicey's decision to keep things secret until the right time.

But things had changed, for Jaicey and for the Craddocks. The wreck had done that. Even without Jaicey's memory loss, the wreck had changed everything, even between Marla and Jake.

Maybe for that reason, more than the others, it might be time to at least consider confessing the secret to Jake, but the thought made her uneasy. What if she was misjudging both him and his father? What if Jaicey had been right to worry? What if this turned out to be the worst possible time, especially if it came from her instead of Jaicey? Did she want that responsibility?

Marla was relieved to be spared the answer to that question when the brisk sound of bootsteps interrupted her thoughts. She turned just as Jake walked in from the hall that led to the big kitchen in back. Her heart skipped with the thrill of seeing him again, especially when she saw his dark eyes light with an instant smile.

Jake walked straight over and swept her up in a big hug before he drew back long enough to give her a swift kiss that ended abruptly.

"Don't want to get that started too early," he growled against her lips, but then he kissed her again. "Sorry I was late." He released her a little and stepped back, catching her hands in his.

Marla smiled, and it felt uncommonly wide, but then,

she felt a rare happiness over his greeting. "I don't mind," she told him. "I was just looking at your family."

Judd came in then. "You're here," he said to Jake. "Good thing for Miss Marla. She was just about to have to choose whether she wanted to spend time with me or see you."

"Putting her on the spot?"

"You know I can't resist the pretty ones."

Jake looked at Marla. "I thought we might drive out, see if we can pick up cougar tracks before lunch. Maybe pass by the old campground above the creek and see if you can spot any arrowheads. Miss Jenny packed a cooler for us, so we could have lunch anywhere the mood strikes you."

Marla's smile widened. She was thrilled with Jake's excitement, and it set fire to her own. She was going to enjoy herself today, enjoy herself a lot.

They told Judd goodbye, then started for the back of the house. Jake got the cooler and Marla thanked Miss Jenny.

And then they went out the door.

CHAPTER ELEVEN

MARLA'S excitement didn't diminish over the day. Jake had driven her to a couple of the places where he thought she might be able to find arrowheads, and she did. A dozen. She was thrilled by her finds, also picking up a few fossils.

She'd told Jake about her interest in archeology as they'd searched the ground, and her fascination with antiques and artifacts of any kind from earlier times. Jake shared the same interest in old things, and she found out that they subscribed to some of the same magazines and had read some of the same books. Jake had not only traveled to several museums, but he'd also worked on an archeological dig in Montana one summer when he'd been in high school.

From there, they drove to the spot where someone had come across cougar tracks two days before. They got out of the pickup and searched the area until they'd found them. Because the land was fairly flat, Jake made her his lookout, having her watch the tracks from the passenger seat so she could direct him as he steered.

They ended up in a hilly area, and since it was lunchtime, they left the trail to cut across country to the nearest creek for lunch. They went wading after they ate.

"This feels so good," Marla said as she swished into the narrow stream. Jake brought the pair of lawn chairs they'd been sitting on, and now he set them in the water, taking a moment for each to make sure they were resting solidly on the bottom.

Barefoot as she was, with his jeans legs rolled up, Jake sat down first, but when she waded closer to her chair, he caught her and set her on his lap. Her feet dangled in the water just to the side of his ankles.

"You're a lightweight, Marlie," he said, grinning.

Marla felt completely at ease putting her arms around his neck. "Thank you for asking me to come out here today."

"You've enjoyed this?" he asked, disbelieving. "We haven't done much yet."

She smiled. "I've loved it. It's easy and peaceful. I hope you won't take it wrong, but it's like being a kid who can just wander around and do what he wants. Be lazy, if he feels like it."

"It's not like this every day out here," he said. "Most of the time, it's hot, hard work, but you've been out here often enough to have seen some of that."

"I like this better than work."

"I'd like it better than your work, too. I couldn't be

cooped up all day in an office like you are. Ever think about doing something else, or are you a career woman?" She smiled wryly.

"I work because I like to eat," she said, then took a small chance. "I started working for a law office the summer before my senior year, and after I graduated, I went to business college and worked part-time there until I finished and went back to the law firm to work full-time. Then I moved to Coulter City and found another law office. I haven't been very adventurous in my job choices." Or in much of anything else, and that gave her a pang that surprised her.

"What do your mama and daddy do for a living?"

It was a natural question, but Marla felt a nettle of tension as she answered. "My adoptive parents were good people," she said as casually as she could. "My father worked in retail, and my mom was a housewife."

"So you're adopted, too. Does Jaicey know that?"

Marla felt a little relieved that Jake had taken that so easily. The fact that he asked if Jaicey knew could be the opening she needed to tell him things that he could mention to Jaicey, but he'd missed her hint that her adoptive parents were no longer living.

"Being adopted is one of the biggest things we've got in common." Marla all but held her breath, expecting him to ask what else they had in common, but Jake appeared oblivious to the lead she'd given him.

"What did your parents think of you moving down here?"

Marla's tension twisted tighter. He was more interested in her than he was in her connection to Jaicey. She'd expected that he might be sometime, if things went on between them, but something told her he meant to zero in on her now. And when it came right down to it, she'd been silent about her past too long to not be nervous about confiding in him. It didn't help that she'd suddenly felt tension in him, too.

"They passed away when I was young," she finally said. "I was a foster child until I graduated high school."

Jake frowned, and her tension shot higher until he said, "You didn't have relatives who took you in?" She could tell he didn't approve of the idea of family not stepping in, and she felt a little relieved.

"There were only two, one from each side of the family. One was elderly, and the other wasn't in the best of health. I was almost eight, so they thought it was better for me to be in a family."

"I'm sorry," he said, and she could see he meant it. "Did the foster family work out then?"

Oh, he'd asked that so gently, as if he suspected it hadn't. But she saw no rejection, no disapproval of her, and no sign yet that he'd think less of her if he knew the truth.

"The first one was good, but the mom got pregnant and had complications, so I was put in another home."

Jake searched her gaze for a few moments, and she had a hard time allowing it. She was losing her nerve, but she'd come here today to take a chance on him. Part of taking a chance on him would also mean that sometime she'd have to let him know a few things about her background. She just hadn't expected it to start this soon or go so quickly to the worst things. On the other hand, maybe it was good for him to know now. She'd find out if he'd still want to see her, so that question would be solved.

"That one was especially bad," she said quietly.

His arm tightened around her. "I'm sorry," he said again. His dark gaze watched hers as he asked, "Was that where you learned to be afraid of men who show anger?"

Her heart gave a hard thud then almost stopped when he added, "Like when you thought I might be out of control and would hurt the kittens?"

Her pent-up breath gusted out on a rush of emotion. He'd gone right for the jugular, straight to one of the most traumatic periods of her life, next to losing her parents. She bit her lip hard to hold back the feelings that had burst up, but his rugged face blurred anyway and she blinked hard to clear her eyes of tears.

He probably did deserve an explanation for her reaction. And he'd asked straight out, so there was no way to avoid this outside of telling him to mind his own business. And part of her wanted him to know; she'd realized that last night. It was just that thinking about doing it, and actually doing it, were vastly different things. Somehow she scraped up the courage.

"That foster father was a cousin of my social worker at the time. I found out there are a few bad apples doing foster care, who get into it for the extra money. Not that there's much money to it, but when you buy thrift shop clothes and apply for every social program you can, and it doesn't bother you if a child has to make do without a lot of things, I guess it's possible to make a profit." She shrugged awkwardly. "And there are some social workers who just want to clear their desk, and see every child as a problem they want to stick somewhere."

Marla had to pause a moment to push down her anger over that. There were good foster parents, a lot of them, just not some she'd had. And though the two social workers she'd had later had done their best, her first social worker had been a bad one. Marla's complaints about abuse had been ignored and, she suspected, had never been officially reported.

"Anyway, that foster dad liked to hit children and kick little animals when he got angry," she pushed herself to say. "So yesterday, I panicked. I was already upset over the snakes. Your anger wasn't out of line or irrational or that bad, but I wasn't thinking, I just reacted. *Over*reacted. I'm sure I offended you, and I'm sorry. The only thing the two of you have in common, is that you're both male."

She thought that would be the end of it, and the limit of what he'd expect her to reveal, but it wasn't.

"So what did the bastard do?"

Nerves made Marla laugh a little at the swear word, but it was more because he'd assigned the monster a slur than because she approved of bad language. Still, she wasn't sure she wanted to tell him much more, so she said, "He'd get drunk, and then he'd get angry. When he was angry, he had to have an outlet. He wasn't man enough to pick on someone his own size."

"Did he hit you? Hurt you?"

Marla couldn't look at him. "Yes, but you learn to stay out of the way."

"You mentioned small animals."

Marla panicked a little at his persistence, but told him. "His kids had a puppy, who was never fast enough to get out of the way." She felt his arms tighten again, and felt more tears sting her eyes. "Let's just say there came a day when the puppy was free and I was free, and another foster kid, Tommy, was free. The monster and his wife were arrested, and I got to testify against them in court."

"I'm sorry, Marlie. I hope the judge threw the book at 'em."

The fierce way he said that made her eyes sting harder, and she was forced to put a stop to it. "There you go again. I had no idea when I met you that you were so relentlessly nice."

"Yeah, and nice makes you cry. I can see those eyes burnin'." Jake shook his head playfully and that made her give him a wobbly smile. "Would it help to tell you a joke?"

That surprised a giggle out of her. "Sure."

"I'll let you know when I think of one," he said, then wrapped his arms tight around her. Marla rested her chin on his shoulder and leaned her head against the side of his as her arms loosely encircled his shoulders. He stroked a hand up and down her back and Marla relaxed.

The stinging in her eyes stopped. She closed her eyes to listen to the gurgling sound of the stream and count the different kinds of chirps from the birds in the trees that overhung this part of the creek. After a few minutes of complete relaxation, she heard Jake's intake of air, and then he spoke.

"Thanks for telling me a little about yourself," he said, his low voice a gravelly drawl. "I like you, Marla Norris, maybe more than like."

Marla's heart quivered, then tipped that last little bit and she felt the long, dangerous fall into love. Not even the reminder that this was too soon made a difference or slowed the descent.

She loved him.

And he liked her! He'd said, *Maybe more than like. Maybe*. The joy she felt was far out of proportion to his quiet declaration, but it was guilt rather than common sense that brought her quickly back to earth.

He liked her. What she'd told him about herself hadn't put him off. But would he still like her if he knew what she'd been keeping from him all this time? Would he understand it if, after she'd told him about a dark time in her life, she *hadn't* told him something that would be even more important to him personally? Something as important to him as the fact that she was his adopted sister's twin, but she was keeping it a secret from him?

She thought again about that wall of family pictures.

Jake understood about family, *his* family, but would he understand that Jaicey had needed to know about her birth family? And even if he was wonderful enough to understand Jaicey and accepted that she'd had to do it, Marla wasn't so sure he'd be as understanding of her for keeping Jaicey's secret for so long, especially after the wreck. And after today...

Now she was in his arms, sitting on his lap, and he didn't have a clue. If Jaicey was suddenly able to remember everything and knew what was going on between her and Jake at this very moment, would she say it was all right, that things had changed too radically between her and Jake for Marla to keep it from him any longer?

The dilemma was making her frantic inside, but the risk of telling or not telling had finally come even with each other. Conscience prodded her so she said a hasty prayer, then reluctantly lifted her head and drew back enough to look into Jake's eyes.

He smiled at her and his gaze fell to her lips. He was about to kiss her, so she put her fingers lightly over his lips. He kissed her fingers, then frowned a little when she took them away.

"What's wrong?" She could see his concern, and saw that it was all for her. Her heart feasted on it.

Oh, how could she tell him and risk losing this? Her heart was greedy for his attention, for his comfort, for his love. She didn't want to throw this all away, this and any future they might have had, even if it was destined to last only a few days or weeks.

Jake's brows came together a little as his concern for her deepened, and a wave of sadness drowned out her selfish cravings. What kind of future could they have, however short, if he didn't find out from her now?

"Jake," she said, her voice all but choked, "there's something I've got to tell you."

One tear then two shot down her cheeks. She lifted her fingers to his jaw, touching him for maybe one of the last times he'd allow it, loving that his skin was faintly rough. He was the kind of man who might need to shave more than once a day, she thought a little hysterically, then tried again to speak.

"I've got to tell you about—"

A sob snatched the rest of that away, and she tried again, but another sob jerked out of her. "I've been keeping this—you need to kn-no—"

Jake lifted a hand to her head to stroke her hair. "Shh, it's okay. Slow down, give yourself time, darlin'. There's no rush."

Frustrated with herself, relieved, and so in love with him she couldn't bear it, Marla broke down completely then, unable to say or do anything but cry, and burrow deeper against him.

Jake's chest rumbled softly as he said, "That's right, cry." He urged her on. "Don't hold back anymore, you've earned it, darlin'."

The guilt she felt about selfishly soaking up his sympathy and comfort made her cry harder and longer, until she felt drained. Heaven knew how long she'd gone on, but Jake hadn't given one indication that he'd grown weary of her breakdown or that he was impatient with it.

And now that the storm was over, he pressed kisses into her hair. Marla loved it, loved him, and wondered what to do now.

After a while, Jake said, "I don't want to see any bashful looks from you, Marlie. Those waterworks only bothered me because you've been hurting too long."

His understanding shamed her and Marla started to draw back to protest, but Jake's arms tightened again to keep her there.

"I like being with you," he growled as he pressed a kiss to her shoulder. "I'd play hooky from work with you anytime, just let me know what day. We can get up to all kinds of fun things, maybe go someplace for the day. I can teach you how to shoot skeet."

He was changing the subject, moving them away from her crying jag, and she realized her opportunity was gone. She lifted her head and this time he let her draw back to look at him. She realized she needed to play along.

"H-how did you know?" She wasn't very good at this, but he ignored her stuttering try and grinned, though his gaze moved tenderly on her flushed face.

"How did I know what? That you wanted to learn how to use a gun and shoot skeet?"

Marla smiled a little then, drawn to this playful side of him. "That I think about playing hooky from work?"

"I know you're a no-nonsense kind of girl, so of course you'd only *think* about playing hooky. If I had your job, I'd not only think about playing hooky, I'd do it at least every other day."

"Is that how you run this ranch?"

"Nope, I like hard work, but I like other things, too." He gave her a long look. "Right now, I'd have to say kissing you again is the thing I like most. So far."

Marla had been enjoying the lazy sound of his voice and grappling with the idea that little more than five minutes ago, she'd been crying her eyes out, when he'd said that. She suddenly thought the world just might have some magic in it after all, and she felt a stir of spirit.

"I think I'd rather you didn't just talk about it."

A slow, sexy smile crossed Jake's handsome face. "Take my hat off, darlin', and toss it to the bank, would you?"

Marla gripped his hat brim, then took it off and tossed it like a Frisbee. He pulled her close.

"Kiss me quick…because something's wrong with this chair."

Marla heard the "kiss me quick" part but his lips touched hers so suddenly that the rest was partly muffled against her mouth.

The kiss was indeed quick, ending on a gasp and a shout of "Whoa!" as the lawn chair jerked to the side, then started to twist. Marla's automatic move to slide off

Jake's lap shifted their weight even more, and drove the chair onto its side.

They were instantly soaked, Jake far more than she as he maneuvered his way out of the chair then sat in the part of the water that was waist high. He raised his knees and rested his elbows on them as he looked down at his sodden clothes. Marla had been lucky enough to only get her jeans legs wet.

Jake's face had gone the color of dark red brick beneath his tan, and his neck looked flushed. The baffled look on his face as he looked down at himself, then at the chair, was priceless, and Marla stood with her hands clapped over her mouth to smother her laughter.

After several stunned moments, Marla had a coughing spasm. Jake slowly looked up at her, noted she was mostly dry, then gave a cranky frown.

"Your hair didn't even get wet."

She could only shake her head and gurgle out a strangled "No," from behind her hands before she abruptly turned away and slogged through the stream to the bank. She wanted to be as far from Jake as she could before the hilarity finally broke loose.

She heard a whoosh and a series of surging swishes before he caught her from behind, and she fell back against him, laughing.

By the time they got back to the ranch house, their clothes had dried. They walked from the pickup hand in hand and Marla felt wonderful. When they came in the back door, Miss Jenny told them Jaicey had been released from the hospital, and was having a late nap. Judd was in the den. After Jake and Marla had some iced tea, Marla decided she needed to go home.

"It'd probably be smart if I go on home," she told him. "I'm not used to being out in the heat and the outdoors, so I'm tired. The kittens could be running low on food by now, too."

"Are you sure?" Jake asked.

She nodded, though it was a disappointment to have the day end without confessing to Jake. The opportunity had passed for now, and she was too worn-out to try again. And Jaicey was here. She'd probably appreciate not having to deal with Marla so soon after the disruption of coming home and the long car ride. Jaicey still wasn't very strong yet, and Marla didn't want to have any more visits that went wrong, especially when they might be the biggest things Jaicey remembered about her so far.

Jake walked her to the car. After he asked to take her to dinner tomorrow night, they said their goodbyes. She was almost grateful that there was no long, steamy kiss. There'd been a few of those today, but the short, sweet one Jake gave her was about all she could handle right now. And then she was driving down away from the ranch house to the highway, feeling a little as if she was driving away from a wonderful dream.

* * *

"Was that Miss Marla leaving?" Judd asked as Jake came into the den. "How come she's rushing off? See if you can call her."

"I don't think she's got a cell phone. And she was tired, not used to being out in all this country air," Jake said, then went to where his sister sat on the sofa and gave her a hug. "Welcome home, stranger."

"I'm glad to be home."

"You look rested," he said as he sat beside her.

"No one bothered me until I woke up on my own." She gave her brother a look. "So you had Marla Norris out for the day. Are you…?"

"Would that make a difference in how you feel toward her?"

Jaicey's gaze shied guiltily from his. "I'm sorry. I keep trying to remember her, and I think there's something important there, but it makes me feel anxious. I'm sorry I hurt her feelings yesterday."

She looked at Jake again. "But if you had her out to visit today, surely she's okay, isn't she, and this is just me?"

"Might not be either one of you," Jake said.

Judd come out from behind the big desk and angled one of the armchairs closer to the coffee table directly across from his children.

As he sat down, he asked Jaicey, "How much do you want to know about Marla?"

The sudden question made both Jaicey and Jake look at him. Jake was sure now that his father had found out something he considered important. He'd wondered about it last night, but he was sure now, and he knew Judd was ready to talk about it.

Jaicey frowned a little. "Everything, I guess. I can't seem to get it on my own, but you've found out something, haven't you?"

"I have." Judd's expression was serious and a little grim. Jake spoke.

"You don't look happy about whatever it is you know. Is that why you asked last night if Marla was adopted?" Jake wasn't sure he approved of this. He felt protective of Marla now.

"I asked if *you* knew she was adopted," Judd said. "And about not looking happy, let's just say I don't like the way I found out, but the idea itself is good. If everything's on the up-and-up, *then* I'd be happy. More than happy."

"So what is it?" Jake asked.

"I can't say I'm one hundred percent, absolutely sure what's true and what isn't, but it looks true to me."

Jaicey looked as if she didn't know what to think, but Jake was intrigued. "How did you find out? Did you call Hodges?"

Hodges was the private investigation agency they'd used in the past. It was expensive, but it was thorough and efficient. The few times they'd had reason to call them in, it had saved them trouble and money.

Judd hadn't answered yet, he was watching Jaicey, so Jake prompted him. "Well?"

"It'd help if Jaicey could remember something about it."

After the lead-in his father had given, it was surprising that he'd suddenly hesitate and look to Jaicey. Jaicey looked blank and a little pale. Jake rescued her.

"So just tell us straight out."

Judd expelled a long breath and leaned back in his chair, still looking at his daughter. "How 'bout it, Jaicey? Are you ready to hear this now, or would you rather wait to see if you can remember on your own later? It's not going to be bad news, unless it's not true. And even then, it won't hurt you."

Jaicey shook her head, then she appeared to change her mind and said a hasty, "Wait…"

Finally she looked at Jake, and with her gaze fixed on his as if to somehow gain strength, she said, "Okay. I want to know."

The room fell silent a few moments. Judd looked at Jake and began.

CHAPTER TWELVE

"Do YOU remember when we adopted Jaicey?" Judd said to Jake. "How sick she was? She'd take in the formula too fast, then she'd choke because it came back up and she'd cry herself blue?"

Jake answered yes, and Jaicey looked at her father, interested in what he'd say. Jake wasn't sure she'd ever heard this. Judd saw her interest and went on.

"Your mama fretted and fussed to put every ounce and quarter inch on that girl. Miss Connie thought they might call it 'reflux' nowadays, and they've got medicine for it now. But back then, doctors didn't see it as much, and maybe they called it colic, at least some of it.

"You grew out of it later, Jaice, but in the beginning, you were hard to adopt because you had a medical problem. The first set of adoptive parents couldn't deal with it and gave you back to the agency. So your mama and I went to see you."

Judd relaxed and smiled then. "Your mama was hoppin' mad that someone would give back a sick baby, so she made up her mind we were going to take you, no matter what. I didn't say so at the time, but I was scared to death you'd die on us. My knees knocked at the idea of getting a baby who'd die and break your mama's heart, but the minute I laid eyes on you, I was willing to fight the devil himself to raise you."

Judd stopped a few moments, not looking at either of them now, his slight smile and faraway look telling Jake he was lost in fond memories. Jake remembered when they'd brought Jaicey home and his mama had put the scrawny, bald baby in his arms.

Little Jaicey had stared up at him, looking him over for a while and then, as if she'd decided she liked him, she'd grinned the kind of toothless, openmouthed grin only babies can do, and gave a little gurgle of delight.

Struck with wonder and surprised to think she liked him already, he'd laughed, too, unable to imagine how a mom and dad could just give her back, like a puppy they'd found out was too much bother. Sure she'd been scrawny and too little for her age, and didn't have a single hair on her head, but she was sweet and soft, and he'd liked the baby powder smell of her. He found out pretty quick that she could also scream the house down at mealtime, but she'd done it so often he'd got used to it.

He'd been proud such a delicate little thing could demand so much attention, that she could outscream a banshee, that she had spunk and spirit and a will to survive. He'd been proud to be her big brother and protector, and he'd doted on her like his mama and daddy had.

Jake had told Jaicey the story years ago and many times since, but he was almost sorry to have more of those memories interrupted when his father went on, but he listened.

"Folks couldn't get much information about the birth families back then, but we were able to get some because you had your medical problem. It was just before the adoption was final that we found out you'd been born with a healthy twin sister. She'd been adopted when you were both a day old."

The information was so unexpected that it took several moments to comprehend. Jaicey had a twin? Jake couldn't remember ever hearing that.

As if his father knew what he was thinking, he added, "We didn't tell you about the twin, because your mama was upset about the babies being separated, as if they weren't worth more than a puppy litter, and she thought it would upset you, too. Then after a while, we were so glad to have Jaicey finally get well and be healthy and happy and growing, that something we couldn't do anything about stopped being important."

Jaicey shook her head as if the news had stunned her. "I had a twin?"

"You did," Judd said, then corrected himself, "you *do*. Does that shake anything loose in your memory?" Jaicey looked dazed.

"How could I remember something from birth?"

Judd chuckled and got up to open the leather satchel on the desk. He lifted out what looked like either a photo album or a scrapbook, and brought it back. He handed it to Jake then sat down.

"That's the photo album that was in Jaicey's wrecked briefcase. That's why I asked you if Miss Marla was adopted."

Judd addressed Jaicey. "Of course you wouldn't remember something from birth, but you and Marla have been close the past few months. That's what I was hoping you'd remember. And you had that album with you in the wreck. You'd just come from Marla's place."

Judd pointed toward the album. "Both of you have a look and tell me who you think Miss Marla's family might be."

Jake felt the enormity of the shock that was coming and his first impulse was to shield his sister. "Are you sure she should just see this?"

"She'd see it anyway if she just happened across it sometime and opened it. At least she's got some clue there's a surprise coming." Judd looked at Jaicey. "You don't need to see it now if you're scared to."

Jaicey shook her head. "No. I've got to see it now. Open it."

Jake positioned the album on his thigh so Jaicey could see it, too. Then he opened it. Jaicey gasped.

The first page read:

Our Lives So Far…
A Brief History of Texas Twins

Jake could hear his sister's voice in the way it was worded, and his chest went tight as he turned the page and saw Jaicey's full name, date of birth, time of day and infant statistics, neatly printed above the hospital photograph of a bald, hours old baby Jaicey. He recognized Jaicey's style of handprinting.

He hadn't let himself look at the right hand page until he'd looked at everything on the left, but it was all but waving at him in his peripheral vision. Then he glanced over and read Marla's name neatly printed with the same list of information, but printed in what must have been Marla's handwriting. Her hospital photo showed that she'd had wispy dark hair, but strikingly similar features to Jaicey's baby picture.

His shock deepened as he paged through the album. He forgot Jaicey sat beside him. Her pictures and the captions about them were always on the left, and Marla's were always on the right. There were more photos of Jaicey, but they must have taken a million of her when she was growing up.

There were a lot fewer of Marla, and though several of Jaicey's included his family and some old proofs of professional family photos, there seemed to be no consistent family photos of Marla with the same family after a certain age, and everything but school photos were snapshots.

He watched both sisters grow older and more different in looks as he turned the pages, until Jaicey and Marla finally looked as unalike as any other two children. When he came to their high school graduation photos, he noted Marla had had the usual professional ones done. When he compared hers side by side with Jaicey's, it was a little easier to see a few vague facial similarities, but nothing that jumped out.

The photos he paged through after the graduation photos had been professionally done by a local studio. And they were very recent, maybe not much more than a couple months old. The last of those were a small three by five selection of the two of them together in front of different scenery with different poses. The two of them must have spent a fortune buying the professional pictures.

The last two pages were photos they'd taken of each other or had someone take of them. Photos from a rodeo, photos at the ranch. Photos of them going on a double date...

Jake let out a long sigh and stared at the last photo of Marla and Jaicey, too stunned to say anything for a few moments. His father had slumped down a little in his chair with his long legs stretched out, and his hands folded over his middle as if he was perfectly relaxed. He looked satisfied by Jake's reaction and looked at his daughter.

Jaicey tried to pull the album off Jake's lap and onto hers, so he moved it for her and held it as he studied her face.

"Are you all right, sis?"

She didn't answer right away, but paged back through the album with her cast-free hand, touching pages, peering at the photos of Marla.

Jake looked over at Judd, who said to him, "Fills in a lot of blanks for me. How 'bout you?"

Before Jake could answer, Jaicey started to cry.

Marla fed the kittens that night—she'd decided to name them Mickey and Samantha, because she wanted to call the little girl Sammy—took her shower, then got her things ready for the next day. By the time the sun went down at nine, she was in bed asleep, with the kittens safely settled in the bathroom with enough dry food and water to last the night. Marla slept deeply, then woke up to the thought that Jake was coming to take her to dinner tonight. She couldn't help being excited.

Once she'd fed the kittens canned food and formula, she got dressed for the day, made a quick list of things she needed to do this week, then took a few minutes to play with the babies. That's when she let herself think about yesterday more fully, remembering that instead of telling Jake what she should have told him, she'd broken down and treated him to a crying jag.

Surely she could find some way to tell him tonight, especially now that she was fairly certain she could tell him without breaking down again. It was hard to believe that she had any tears left, but she'd felt that way before. And Jake was too important to her. His respect was important to her. She didn't want to come this far with him and then have it come to nothing. She didn't want him to hate her. Please God...

She'd finally closed the babies in the bathroom for the day, got her handbag and opened the hall door, when she heard a knock on the glass of the patio door. The drapes were closed, and it was seven-thirty in the morning, so she had no idea who it could be. Marla closed the hall door, set her handbag on the entry table, then crossed to the far end of the living room to peek out from between the drapes.

To her surprise, Jake stood on her small patio, his expression grim. She jerked back her hand and let the drapes close in a childish attempt to keep from being seen. But the moment she'd peeked out, her gaze had collided with his.

He'd looked grim, and she'd not read a thing in his eyes except intensity, and yet she somehow knew he'd found out about the secret. It took her a long moment to brace herself before she reached for the cord and opened the drapes.

Jake looked like a giant about to step into a child's play house again. Guilt and dread make him seem even larger and more intimidating this time. He wore a stark white shirt and dark jeans, with the same black boots polished to a muted shine and his black Stetson. She rolled the bar out of the track, unlocked the slider and started to open it when his big hand slipped through the space she'd made and opened it for her.

Marla stepped back and waited out of the way as he tugged the slider and it hissed closed. She dared a look up into his face, trying to remember she deserved whatever he would say to her now. She should never have agreed to Jaicey's secret, and even though she had, she shouldn't have allowed it to drag out this long. She should have found some way to tell Jake the whole story yesterday, no matter how long it had taken her to get over her crying jag, no matter how quickly he'd tried to move her to happier thoughts.

"Jaicey and I had a look at her album last night, and I understand you have one just like it," he said without preamble.

He didn't sound or even look angry exactly, he was just somber, and somehow that was worse. Did that mean he was disappointed in her as well as angry? That made two of them. She was disappointed in herself, too. She should have told him all of it. Maybe she could have eased him into it. Maybe what she was seeing on his face was what remained of getting a shock.

Then she realized what else he'd said and felt her heart lift a little. "Jaicey got her memory back?" He nodded.

"Seeing the album did it. She had a lot of explaining to do."

"Was your father upset?"

"Only that she'd hidden it from him."

Marla felt the first glimmers of relief, but Jake still looked grim. "I hid it, too," she reminded him. It was a puny confession, but that was the only one left to her.

Jake took his Stetson off then. "I know you did."

He tossed it to one of the armchairs behind her, because she heard the soft sound as it landed. "It says something that you were loyal enough to Jaicey to keep the secret, even though it meant you were cut out of her life for a while. But then yesterday you meant to tell me, but I wouldn't let you, even when you tried a second time."

Marla gave a small nod, "Yes. I'm sorry. I thought I could, but by the time I convinced myself things had changed between us, and I shouldn't keep it from you, it was too emotional to tell. Then you seemed to want to move on, but I used that as an excuse not to try again. I could have insisted that second time, and I should have."

The admission brought those emotions back as if they'd never found release, but she harshly forced them back. She'd rather drown in her tears than let them show now and have Jake think they were a bid for mercy.

"I would have thought you'd show less emotion over telling me about Jaicey than you did over your foster father. Instead the idea of telling me who you really are was either the straw that broke the camel's back, or you were more upset about telling me your secret."

Marla's gaze fled his, not able to understand why he

was pursuing this as she scrambled for something to say to that, something other than, "I was afraid I'd lose you." She made herself look up at him.

"That's easy. The foster homes are many years past, but telling you was a 'here and now' thing. Especially after you'd been so nice to me and maybe become sort of a friend."

Marla cringed inwardly, and all of a sudden she felt pitiful, and about as transparent as glass. Why not admit the truth, or at least as much of the truth as her pride allowed?

"I'm not made of stone, you know," she said in a quiet voice. "What man wouldn't want to keep things going with you?" She took a breath and held it a moment. His dark eyes were intent on her, and she felt achingly self-conscious. "So where does that leave us?"

"That leaves us about two feet too many apart, Miss Marlie."

His sudden answer jolted her, and the word, "What?" practically fell from her lips.

And then he swept her up in his arms and his lips landed firmly on her open ones. Her body went so weak she was surprised she didn't faint, but a woman who'd fainted couldn't feel the things she was as her arms went around his neck and she hung on for dear life.

Jake was kissing her, turning her insides to mush, sending her blood pounding through her veins in a wild rhythm that pounded out a cadence that sounded a lot like, He loves me, he loves me. When he finally drew back, his dark eyes glittered down at her.

"Daddy should be at your office by now. He's going to pass along the message that you aren't coming into work today, because you and I have a lot to do," he said but Marla's head was still spinning from that kiss and it took her a few moments to comprehend what he'd said.

"What do we have to do?" she asked.

"We have to make plans, buy rings, and Jaicey can't wait to see you again."

Marla felt as if she'd stepped off a cliff and was falling through space. Any minute, she'd hit the ground and she'd realize this was a crazy dream. Or Jake was making a very bad joke.

"Wait," she said. "I get the part about Jaicey, but the rest?" She couldn't repeat words he'd said.

Jake smiled down at her. "We've got plans to make today. If you won't make them with me today, I'll come back tomorrow, or the next day or the next. Every day until next Monday, and if you still won't agree to marry me, then I'll start coming back every day for another week."

Marla's heart went into that wild rhythm again, and joy began to unfurl. However stupid it sounded, Marla had to ask. She had to be sure. "Why? Why would you do that?"

"Because I love you, Marlie. I'm not even sure when it happened, whether it was early on or yesterday. But

I knew it the moment I opened that photo album and found out who you are, and realized what I hadn't let you tell me at the creek. After I got past some of the shock, my first coherent thoughts were, 'Will she marry me?' and 'I wonder if twins will run in the family.'"

Marla's heart was still stuck on the part about Jake loving her, but her brain was afraid to believe it. And then Jake went solemn again. "Do you love me yet? I know this is soon, and I'd understand if you'd prefer a proper courtship. Your life has been pretty radical lately, moving to Texas, getting to know Jaicey better, dealing with a new home, a new job, the wreck…"

The list trailed off, giving Marla an opportunity to answer. "Yes. I do…love you," she said, then felt emotional. "I thought I'd never say that to any man, much less to you, but I do love you." Jake frowned playfully.

"You look mighty surprised about that, and I'm not sure it's a compliment. I always thought I was lovable."

Marla giggled. "It's a compliment. I didn't think I'd ever say that to anyone because I didn't believe I could love, or if I did, I could never risk saying it. But I love you." She laughed a little. "I love you. Oh, it feels so good to know it—to feel it like this—and to feel free to say it."

This time, she pulled him down and kissed him, and he caught her up and blindly carried her across the living room and down the hall because he didn't break the kiss until he stopped outside the bathroom door.

He drew back enough to rasp, "I assume the kittens are

in here?" Marla got out a breathless yes. "Then open the door so they can come out. I've got a feeling things between us might get a little involved, and you'll need them."

"Need them?" she asked.

"As an excuse to cool things off," he growled, "and show me the door when my time's up."

Marla smiled. "You noticed that the other evening?"

"I've been takin' notes on everything about you, Miss Marlie. And, if I can stand it, I want to wait for our wedding night, as long as that night isn't too far away."

And then he glanced down at the floor, making sure the kittens weren't underfoot before he carried her back to the living room and sat down on the middle cushion with her on his lap. Then he kissed her again, and neither of them noticed anything but each other for a while.

Later, Marla's head rested contentedly against Jake's shoulder. While they talked and made plans for their future, the kittens climbed up the leg of Jake's jeans to listen and find a comfortable spot for their nap.

If you enjoyed what you just read,
then we've got an offer you can't resist!

Take 2 bestselling
love stories FREE!

Plus get a FREE surprise gift!

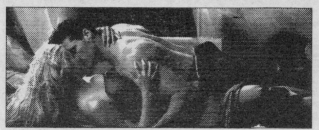

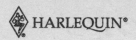

HARLEQUIN®

HARLEQUIN ROMANCE®

Coming Next Month

#3883 HER ITALIAN BOSS'S AGENDA Lucy Gordon
The Rinucci Brothers

Olympia Lincoln is so relieved when her new assistant shows up that she sets him to work immediately. What she doesn't realize is that he is none other than Primo Rinucci, her new Italian boss! Primo can't resist playing along with the harmless deception—after all, this way he can get really close to the beautiful Olympia....

#3884 PRINCESS OF CONVENIENCE Marion Lennox
Heart to Heart

Raoul needs a bride—fast!—if he's to be Prince Regent of Alp'Azuri. His country's future is at stake—and so is his nephew's life. Beautiful and vulnerable Jessica agrees to marry him, but must return to Australia the next day. She could all too easily risk her heart in a place like Alp'Azuri, married to man like Raoul....

#3885 THE MARRIAGE MIRACLE Liz Fielding

Matilda Lang is terrified when she finds herself falling for hotshot New York banker Sebastian Wolseley. An accident three years ago has left her in a wheelchair, and Sebastian is the man who can make—or break—her heart. It would take a miracle for Matty to risk her heart after what she's been through, but Sebastian knows he can help her....

#3886 HER SECRET, HIS SON Barbara Hannay

When Mary Cameron left Australia she was carrying a secret— a secret she's kept to herself for years. But now Tom Pirelli is back, and she's forced to confront the choices she made. It's Mary's chance to tell Tom the real reason she left him—and that he's the father of her child...!